Elope to Death

A RINEHART SUSPENSE NOVEL

RINEHART SUSPENSE NOVELS

BY JOHN CREASEY AS GORDON ASHE

A Plague of Demons

A Shadow of Death

A Blast of Trumpets

The Big Call

A Herald of Doom

Murder with Mushrooms

A Life for a Death

The Croaker

A Rabble of Rebels

Wait for Death

A Nest of Traitors

The Kidnaped Child

A Scream of Murder

Double for Death

A Clutch of Coppers

Death from Below

A Taste of Treasure

A RINEHART SUSPENSE NOVEL

John Creasey

as Gordon Ashe

Elope to Death

HOLT, RINEHART AND WINSTON
New York

Published simultaneously in Canada by Holt,
Rinehart and Winston of Canada, Limited.

Library of Congress Cataloging in Publication Data
Creasey, John.
Elope to death.
(A Rinehart suspense novel)
I. Title.
PZ3.C86153El8 [PR6005.R517] 823'.9'12 76-43493
ISBN 0-03-020621-9

First published in the United States in 1977.

Printed in the United States of America

10 9 8 7 6 5 4 3 2 1

Contents

1	Now or Never	7
2	Decision	16
3	Distress	23
4	Gillian's Mother	30
5	More Cause for Alarm	37
6	Ceremony	45
7	Message	53
8	Luck?	60
9	"Accident"	68
10	Facilities	75
11	Second Change	84
12	Need for Haste	92
13	Three Birds	99
14	Secret	106
15	Night Rides	113
16	Monet	120
17	First Alarm	128
18	Questions	135
19	Sharp	144
20	Tactics	150
21	Passport	157
22	Heat	164
23	Over	171
24	Hidden Factor	179
25	Future . . .	186

Elope to Death

A RINEHART SUSPENSE NOVEL

1

Now or Never

GILLIAN did not notice the way Clive was looking at her, only the way he held her arm and guided her, as if he knew exactly how to make her miss the puddles. Laughing, a little breathless, plastic-hat-cover tied under her chin, she reached the pavement. A man with an umbrella held low in front of him against the beating rain, loomed up; Clive side-stepped and missed him.

They reached the corner of a narrow turning, the uneven flagstones streaming with water, and Gillian had to pick her way on her high-heeled shoes until they came to a runway which was overflowing from an overloaded pipe.

'Now you are beaten!' she declared.

'Am I?' Clive asked, and lifted her with a single swift movement, carried her over the stream and placed her on comparatively dry land. For a moment they stood close together; and then he took her in his arms again and kissed her.

'You'll never know how much I love you,' he said.

She knew how her own heart was pounding; how, after a few days, this man had meant more to her than anyone she had ever met. She was oblivious of people passing the end of the alley, but strained against him, and the strength in his arms seemed great enough to crush her.

He let her go.

'This way,' he said gruffly, and took her arm. The rain splashed up from the rounded cobbles, and the narrow confines of the little yard made it hiss and siss. Only fifty yards away was the hustle of London's traffic in the Strand, the roar, the hideous hoardings of twentieth-century progress; yet here was a corner of a London three hundred years old, with low buildings and red-tiled, uneven roofs, bottle glass in some of the windows, small doors which did not seem to fit. Brass plates were everywhere announcing lawyers, accounts, a dentist and an antiquarian bookshop, all very subdued and dignified. So was the restaurant in the corner, with meringues piled up in the small window. Clive guided Gillian towards it, and the door was opened as they approached by a girl.

'Good-afternoon,' she greeted. 'Isn't the weather dreadful?'

'Gets worse every day,' Clive answered. He smiled at the girl, and she stared at him as most young girls did; because there were few men more handsome. He shook his umbrella out, and the girl said:

'Let me take that, sir—and shall I take the lady's coat and hat?'

'You call that a hat?' Clive scoffed.

Gillian laughed and so did the girl; it was easy to laugh with Clive. Water streamed off the plastic on to the mat at the shop doorway, and a trickle ran up Gillian's sleeve.

'Is there room upstairs?' Clive asked the girl.

'Yes, sir.'

'Fine.' Clive took Gillian's arm again, and guided her along a narrow passage. Doors on either side showed tables mostly filled, girls in their blue smocks with puff sleeves serving teas as if they were part of that earlier century. At the end of the passage was a twisting staircase with narrow, uneven treads, a wooden wall on one side, and open banisters on the other. There was no need for Clive's supporting hand, and yet Gillian was glad of it. At the landing it was very different; a passage led between alcoves with high-backed benches, each cushioned; and each alcove had comfortable room for two, facing each other. They came to an empty one.

'Ours,' Clive said. 'You sit this side; it's a nicer view.'

'It's a charming place.'

'Ye Olde Worlde,' Clive said.

'Don't scoff at it.'

'It's the last thing I'd do,' he assured her. She had to push her way between the table and the edge of the seat, but once she was sitting down there was plenty of room. Rain smacked against the window, but did not hide her view of the old courtyard. Clive looked at her curiously. 'Old things don't really attract you, do they?'

'Not like they do my mother,' Gillian said. 'Or you, for that matter. Oh, I like them, but there's so much faking done. Only a week or two ago I was looking at a so-called Louis Quinze chair which had a broken leg, and found that a new leg had been put on some time ago. The wood was actually hollow, and someone had used it for smuggling, I think.'

'Smuggling?' Clive's voice was sharp. 'Are you sure?'

'Well, there were two metal cylinders inside it, which could have held jewels or anything small,' Gillian told him. 'I showed it to Mother, and she pretended to laugh, but I could see it sickened her.'

'If she hates fakes or false legs like that, she's really an antique lover,' Clive said. 'Like to hear an awful confession, sweet?'

'I don't know.'

'I'm not a lover of old things for their own sake,' Clive told her. 'I work for one of the best firms in Europe, with connections everywhere, and I suppose I know as much about them as most men in the trade, but—well, the fake stuff *does* sicken me. Let's change the subject! You'd be surprised how greatly any special customers are impressed by this little bit of old England. Dozens of Europeans, Americans, Canadians, Australians and South Africans have sat there, not to mention New Zealanders and—but I'll spare you the whole list.' He stretched out his hand and gripped hers. 'This place is part of my life, darling, as I hope you will soon be.'

She didn't speak.

He was so very English to look at, clear-skinned, fair-haired; she had always imagined Clives to be dark, whereas he was a typical Saxon. It was hard to say why he was so good-looking, it was less feature by feature than the general effect. He had a square chin with a hint of a cleft, a rather short, straight nose, the clearest of grey eyes.

'And we'll never have a better chance,' he went on.

Gillian said, 'I know.'

'After all,' Clive observed, 'it won't be the first time that a mother's favourite daughter has eloped.'

'No.'

'If your mother were in London we could go and see her,' Clive said, 'but there just isn't time to go to Cornwall, and you can hardly talk about this by telephone.' He pressed her hands gently. 'From all you've told me about her, she's as nice as she's understanding, and even if she were upset, I'd win her round.'

'Yes,' Gillian conceded slowly. 'I believe you would.'

'Then why hesitate, sweetheart?' Clive asked, and leaned forward. 'We're in love, we've the opportunity for a honeymoon in the South of France, there'll never be another chance like it.'

One of the girls in a pale-blue smock came up, making Clive turn to look at her; but he did not free Gillian's hands.

'Tea and meringues, please,' Clive said.

'Yes, sir.' The girl went back.

To Gillian, it was rather like a scene in a film, and almost impossible to believe that this was really happening to her. She did not recognize the fierceness of her own emotions, the pounding of her heart, the yearning to do what Clive wanted; to elope, to marry in France, then spend a week or two touring France and another two on the Riviera. It was a dream. But her mother wasn't a dream: she was there in the background, not commanding, but trusting—as she had been ever since Gillian could remember.

'You know as well as I do that she would soon get over it. After all'—Clive went on with a glint of merriment in his eyes—'a mother doesn't often have a chance of acquiring a handsome, well set-up young son-in-law with a job which will enable him to keep his wife in extreme comfort, if not in luxury.'

'Don't joke about her, Clive.'

'My sweet, I couldn't be more serious!'

'You see,' Gillian said, and hesitated before going on more quickly: 'We've always been so close together. It would have been different if father had been alive, but for the past ten years Mother's life has revolved round me.'

'I know.'

'And to desert her like this would hurt her so much.'

'My sweet,' said Clive, still gently, 'there are one or two things you have to face up to. You're a young woman with her own life to lead. You've a great sense of loyalty and gratitude to your mother, but you can't stay with her for the rest of your life. I don't for one moment think she means to dominate you, but at the moment her influence is so great that she's making it very difficult for you to imagine life without her.'

'But she deliberately went away on holiday by herself this year!'

'Yes, I know,' said Clive, and the pressure of his fingers became almost painful. 'That's exactly what I'm driving at. Your mother realizes that she's keeping you too close to her, so she's forced herself to go away for two weeks. She knows very well that sooner or later the parting will come. If it's quick and sharp, it will be easier in the long run. Kinder, too.' He moved back as the waitress arrived, with six snowy-white meringues piled on a large dish, and a small crock of whipped cream to go with them, tea, and some wafer-thin bread and butter.

When the waitress had gone, Clive went on urgently: 'If I hadn't to go away for at least a month I wouldn't try to persuade you, but I've got to start the trip to France tomorrow. I daren't delay it, but I can share the month with you.' He picked up one of the meringues and spread cream on the flat side, thick and oozing. 'That's as good as any you'll get in France or anywhere on the Continent,' he added jerkily. 'Like cream?'

'Love it,' Gillian made herself say.

'I'll tell you what,' Clive said, and forced a smile, 'let's put the problem out of our minds for an hour or so. I have to look in at the office and you've some shopping to do. Supposing we meet again at—say six o'clock.' He glanced at the gold wristwatch. 'It's a little after four now; that's nearly two hours.'

'To decide our whole future,' Gillian said, rather huskily.

'Ah,' said Clive, 'that's the point, sweet. You're not really sure of yourself, are you? Heaven knows I can't blame you, but—don't fool yourself. Don't blame your mother for a decision you're nervous of making yourself.'

'But, Clive . . .' Gillian began, but couldn't finish. They had known each other for less than a month; how could she be absolutely sure of him? How could he be of her? She hated the thought of not seeing him for a month or more, but perhaps that would be wise; perhaps when they met again her heart would not beat so furiously.

'Or if you'd rather have a little more time, why don't you go home, and telephone me, if—if you decide to come?' Clive suggested. He gave the impression that he was fighting against showing his emotions. 'I want it to be your own free decision, my darling. And remember I *am* offering you marriage!'

'I know,' Gillian said huskily. 'Clive, I feel such a beast, but I must think about it. If only there were a few days to decide in, instead of a few hours! Being now or never——'

'If ever there was a need for a snap decision, this is it,' Clive declared. 'But I'm not going to say another word about it. I'll be home all the evening. If you telephone, I'll know you're coming—and God knows I can't tell you how much that will mean to me. If you don't—then I'll call you the moment I'm back from the continent, whether it be in four weeks or in eight. Right, darling?'

She nodded.

'Fine,' said Clive. 'Now, tell me if that isn't the best cream meringue you've ever tasted.'

In fact, she hardly tasted it at all.

When they left the rain had nearly stopped, but the cobbles and the streets were streaming, and the clouds overhead were as heavy as ever. They passed a travel agency with posters in the window, one of them saying simply: *The Riviera for Sunshine.* For the past few weeks there had been rain, clouds, occasional glimpses of the sun, and temperatures fifteen degrees below average for June. Just past the agency was Clive's office. In front of it, he gripped her arm, said fiercely: 'Don't make me wait, darling,' and then turned and strode away.

She almost cried out after him, but watched his square shoulders and his easy movements before he disappeared. Then she turned slowly towards a bus stop, to make the first major decision she had ever made in her life.

. . . . .

Clive Macklin opened the door of the small office on the third floor of the building, and a middle-aged woman sitting at a small desk in front of a typewriter looked at him curiously, and said:

'Good afternoon, Mr. Macklin. Mr. Sharp's in his office.'

Macklin nodded and opened another door, marked *Principal.* The office beyond was small, well-furnished, and had a window overlooking the Strand. It was closed, and traffic noises were muted. Sitting at the only desk was a small, very well-dressed man, who gave the impression that he had been freshly shampooed, manicured and polished. His face was powdered, his greying hair was crimped. He looked up at Macklin without a smile and without expression as he asked:

'Is she going with you?'

'I'll know tonight,' Macklin said.

'She had better go,' the other man remarked quietly. 'She must be out of this country tomorrow, or else she must be dead. I can't take any more risks. Why didn't you make sure she said "yes"?'

'Because she isn't the kind who'll let anyone else make up her mind for her,' Macklin answered. His hands were close by his sides, and he was clenching his fingers. 'I think she'll come.'

'Judging from the look of you, you mean you hope she will,' said the man named Sharp. 'What's on your mind?'

'Nothing,' Macklin answered uneasily.

'Yes there is.' Sharp looked at him levelly. 'Are you falling for her?'

'Of course I'm not.'

'I'm not so sure,' Sharp said softly. 'Macklin, don't get ideas. I want that girl out of the country for at least three weeks, and if you can't get her out she'll have to go the same way as Ivy Marshall. Remember Ivy?'

'There's no need to talk like that,' Macklin protested in a low-pitched voice. 'Ivy knew too much. I can see why she had to go, but this girl——'

'I want this girl out of England because I've got to handle a delicate job which she could spoil. If you want to save her pretty neck, you'd better make sure she goes.'

'I'll get her to come,' Macklin said.

'All right, but get her over to France quickly.' Sharp said. 'You'll pick up details of your itinerary in Paris. Do exactly what you're told if you want to make sure that the police never find out that you killed Ivy Marshall.'

'I'll do what you want,' Macklin said bitterly. 'I've got to, haven't I?'

He left ten minutes afterwards, and had hardly reached the street before Sharp was on the telephone, speaking to a man who had a pronounced French accent.

'Macklin is worrying me,' Sharp said. 'I want to make sure he and this girl are followed until I think the danger's quite past. It might even be necessary to make sure that neither of them comes back,' he added briskly. 'Make sure we always know where they are.'

2

Decision

'IT'S no use,' Gillian said to herself. 'I'll have to telephone Mother.'

She jumped up from the easy chair in the living-room of the Kensington flat which she shared with her mother, glanced at the clock, and saw that it was nearly eight. With luck, her mother would just have finished dinner. The telephone was near the door; she sat on the edge of another chair, dialled, and waited for the long-distance operator. She knew the telephone number of the hotel near Penzance, because she and her mother spent two or three weeks there most years; it had become a family tradition.

She gave the number.

'Hold on, please,' the operator said.

Gillian sat with her ankles crossed, staring across the room at the window. It was open a little at the top, and a gusty wind made the curtains billow. She kept seeing mind pictures of that poster about the Riviera, and superimposed upon it was Clive, turning away from her, gritting his teeth as he forced himself not to plead any more.

What would her mother say?

That she mustn't go, of course. What else was there for her to say? It wasn't as if she knew Clive; if she did, then there was every chance that she would give her blessing, but—how could she agree that it would be a good thing to marry a stranger? That was the fantastic thing: that anyone could think of Clive being a stranger to her. She brushed her dark waving hair back from her forehead. It was very close tonight; thunder was probably about. Once or twice she thought she heard rumbles in the distance. There were noises on the wire, more than usual, and probably due to bad weather. Of course, her mother would say "No," and that would be an end to it. Open defiance was one thing; going off without a word was another.

Was Clive right?

Did her mother recognize the dangers of dominating her too much? Would it be better to make the wrench suddenly, sharply and painfully?

How could she explain over the telephone why she was so positive that he was the right man for her to marry? How could she explain that he was the first man she had known who had respected her absolutely; who hadn't made any kind of pass, who hadn't hinted at the delights of quiet lanes and—oh, Clive was *good.*

Did she want to marry him?

Yes, yes, *yes!* That was the peak of her longing, everything she wanted; when she was with him it was like being with another part of herself.

'Sorry to keep you, but I'm putting you through now,' the operator said. There were different sounds almost muffled by a toll of thunder, and a squall of rain came smashing against the window. Rain, rain, rain, that was all it ever did; Gillian felt that she could do anything to get away, to find some sunshine, to be warm, to be married, to wake up in the morning and find Clive next to her.

'This is the Cliffside Hotel,' a man said, and she recognized the proprietor of the small hotel overlooking one of the loveliest coves of the Cornish coast.

'Is Mrs. Kelvedon there, please?' Gillian asked.

'I think she's gone out,' the man answered. 'Isn't that Miss Kelvedon?'

'Yes.'

'We were so sorry you couldn't get away this year,' the other said. 'It's quite a pleasant evening here for a change. Hold on, and I'll see if your mother's in—I remember hearing some talk of a party going into Penzance to see a film.' He went off, while Gillian stared at the window again. If her mother was out, it would be like a finger of fate.

'Don't be a fool,' she told herself almost savagely. 'You're a big girl now, you're grown-up, you're twenty-three.' Yet if her mother was out, then she would be thrown back on her own resources. The proprietor was away for a long time, and Gillian began to wonder if they had been cut off. She leaned forward so that she could see herself in a mirror, and was startled by the tense look on her face.

'Hallo, Miss Kelvedon!'

Gillian nearly choked. 'Hallo!'

'Your mother's gone into Penzance, and won't be back until about eleven o'clock. Would you like her to telephone you when she gets in?'

'No,' answered Gillian, almost too loudly. 'No, it's all right, I just felt that I'd like a word with her before going to bed.'

'She'll be sorry to have missed you.'

'Yes,' Gillian said. 'I know. Thank you, Mr. Thomas. Good night.' She hardly heard him echo "good night" as she put the receiver down. The earlier feeling, that her decision was really being made for her, came back very strongly. She went to the window and looked out into the rainwashed street; a car passed and its lights showed how the rain was streaming down; and she heard the swish of its wheels through the pools in the road. She turned away sharply, went into her bedroom, and stood in front of the full-length mirror. She still wore the dark blue knitted dress that she had worn this afternoon; winter in June. It was just a little too tight, and emphasized the lines of her figure, the curve of her hips and the curve of her breasts, but it was high at the neck, and there were long sleeves; it was immodestly modest, in a peculiar way. She knew how it attracted men's glances, and she had been wearing this when she had first seen Clive at the Corrisons party. She could not be sure who had introduced them. 'This is Clive, Clive this is Gillian, you two ought to know each other.' They had been left together, smiling a little over-politely, and she had realized that this man was different in looks and in bearing from most, and in manner. She could remember vividly the way he had looked her up and down, actually standing back to do so, and then said:

'You are quite the loveliest girl here. Did you know that?'

She had laughed . . . they had laughed. And she had seen him nearly every night since then. Strangers! In some ways she knew him better than she knew herself. She knew where he had been born, where he had been educated. While at public school he had lost both his parents. She could remember how he had passed that over quickly. She had learned how he had started work at a small antique shop in Guildford, graduated, as he had put it, to London, and now was the European representative of a small London firm of dealers in antiques and fine art. He travelled the Continent, both buying and selling. They had no show-rooms, as all of their business was to the trade; there was no retail side.

'. . . and I act as a kind of universal aunt to all our visiting customers when I'm at home,' he had told her.

That was why he had been at the Corrisons party, of course, and why she had. Her mother ran a small antique shop in Kensington, near the flat, and whenever she came upon a really good piece to sell, she took it to Corrisons, where she could always get a good price. Corrisons was a shop of world-wide fame.

Until Gillian had met Clive, old furniture, even when really beautiful, had not attracted her as it had her mother. But Clive's interests had become hers. He had taken her past Corrisons main display windows several times, and suddenly the shop had been full of the beauty of the past. She could remember some of the miniatures he had pointed out, beautiful sixteenth-century work, and some old jewellery which had been owned by the nobility of France and Italy, Spain and Germany, hundreds of years ago.

And there she stood, with a clinging dress shaping her, her dark hair tousled and a little unruly, her eyes looking more blue because of the pale blue of the ceiling in this room, her skin without a blemish. She was a little exotic to look at, she knew; Gillians should be fair where she was dark, Clives should be dark. . . .

'I must make up my mind!' she exclaimed aloud, and her voice broke. 'He's sitting by the telephone waiting.'

She went back into the living-room.

She thought, "I'll have to go with him, I know I will."

She looked round at the baby grand piano, and at the tinted photograph of her mother; there was a great likeness between them.

Everything she had ever been taught or believed in warned her that it would be wrong to elope, but there was Clive's voice: the twisted smile, as if he had been fighting back emotion; the way he had said that it would be better to get the break over quickly. And it would—there was no doubt about that. This was a chance of her whole life—all the romance and all the wonder of elopement, the journey across the channel, the drive through France, the Riviera . . . a honeymoon in the South of France; Clive with her, every minute of the day and night.

'I can't help it!' she said suddenly, very quiet-voiced. 'I've got to go with him!' She swung round towards the telephone and snatched it up—now that the decision was made—and her fingers were unsteady when she dialled; once she nearly pushed the instrument off its small table. Mayfair 01345 . . . Mayfair, W.1. It was dreamlike, she reminded herself; a husband who lived with beauty, to whom culture was part of life; a husband with plenty of money, a dream. . . .

A husband she loved.

The telephone was ringing, brrr-brrr; brrr-brrr; and it kept ringing. She had expected Clive to be close by, waiting to snatch it up. Why should he be? It was half-past eight, and he had probably given up hope that she would call at all. Yet she was sharply disappointed, and she stood up and stared at the piano and that photograph as the ringing sound went on and on. Where was he? Surely he hadn't gone out. He had said that he would be near the telephone all the evening.

The ringing sound stopped.

'Clive Macklin,' Clive announced, as if he were breathless.

Now that he was at the other end, Gillian could hardly bring herself to speak.

'Clive . . .' she began.

'Gillian!' His whole voice seemed to exult. 'Oh, thank God you've called! I was beginning to fear——' He broke off, and now she could hear that he was breathless. 'I—I had a visit from a neighbour, I was at the front door.'

'It doesn't matter,' Gillian said, and she was almost choking, too. 'Clive, I'm coming.'

'Thank God for it! And, Gillian, you'll never regret it. I swear that you'll never regret it for one moment. Gill, it's wonderful.' He broke off, and Gillian believed that he was as choky as she, and hardly knew what to say.

'Clive, I must see you!'

'I must see *you!* Darling, stay there,' Clive urged, still chokily. 'I'll get the car out and be with you in twenty minutes. Stay right there.'

'Yes,' Gillian said. 'Darling, I—I love you.'

'God, how I love you!' he cried. Then the line went dead, and it seemed incredible that the warmth and vitality of his voice should have been stilled. She stood transfigured for a few moments, then banged down the receiver and ran into her bedroom, opened the wardrobe door, took out three dresses and flung them aside, took out a red lace dress she knew that he liked, slid out of her clothes, sat with only her bra and panties on, stockings taut on her slim legs. She made up swiftly and with the radiance in her eyes, did her hair and slipped into the dress. He had said twenty minutes and would be here on the dot.

She leaned forward towards the mirror, and touched her lashes with a damp middle finger.

She heard a car.

She rushed to the window and looked out, and saw Clive's low-lying Jaguar pulling up outside, saw him get out and without glancing up at the window, dart through the rain towards the house. He couldn't get in! She tore out of the room and into the small hall, pulled the front door open and half ran down the stairs, reaching the bottom as he rang the bell. It was a self-contained first-floor flat, and neighbours would have no idea who had called. If they had, it wouldn't matter.

She opened the door.

Clive stood there with his eyes glowing.

. . . . .

'It's all fixed,' Macklin said into the telephone. 'She's coming.'

'That's more like it,' Sharp approved. 'You will call at the two Paris shops, Fontainebleau, Auxerre, Souillac and Marseilles. If there's any need to change the itinerary, I will send messages in the usual way.'

'Don't forget I'll be on my honeymoon,' Macklin said.

3

Distress

PATRICK DAWLISH stooped to adjust the roto-scythe so that it would cut the grass on the lawn close to the house, and the noise of the engine muffled the sound of everything else, even of the aeroplane which was droning overhead. It was a dry day, with heavy cloud which lifted now and again for the sun to come through. He looked at the great stretch of lawn on either side of the drive, badly overgrown because there had been so little opportunity to get the machine on to it this summer. With luck he would get one side cut tonight, and the other in the morning; unless, of course, it rained. He felt really warm for the first time for weeks, and before he released the brake took out his handkerchief and wiped his forehead and the back of his neck. Doing so, he caught sight of a movement out of the corner of his eye, and realized that Felicity, his wife, was waving out of the drawing-room window. He could see her mouth open, and grinned, for she seemed never to realize that it was impossible for him to hear above the noise of the roto-scythe. He turned it down as far as he could, and then strolled towards her; but his slow gait did not satisfy her, and she beckoned furiously, and formed a word which might have been, '*Hurry!*'

She looked good; fresh and wholesome in anyone's eyes and, in some moments especially, beautiful in his. He waved. She beckoned more furiously, and he realized that it wasn't simply impatience. He quickened his stride, which was already long. He was a very tall, very broad man, massive against the background of trees and, beyond them, green fields and cattle against the cumulus of the clouds. He jumped down on the drive, now equidistant between Felicity and the machine, and heard her call:

'It's Tim!'

'Tim? I don't have to hurry for Tim,' he scoffed.

She turned away as he reached the porch, and when he went inside the hall of the neo-Tudor home with its narrow oak floor, its oak-panelled hall and its charm, he heard her in the living-room, talking.

'. . . he's just coming, it was that awful roto-thing, you can't hear yourself speak . . . Who did you say? . . . Well, here he is, you can speak to him about it yourself.' She held a hand over the mouthpiece and turned to face Dawlish. She was a tall woman, very slim, with between-coloured hair brushed back from her forehead, calm green-grey eyes, and a fresh colouring. 'It's about a Mrs. Kelvedon. Tim says you know her.'

'I certainly do,' said Dawlish. His eyes glowed and he made curvaceous shapes in the air with his hands. 'My, my!' He took the telephone. 'Thanks, sweet. . . . Hallo, Tim, what's this about Kay Kelvedon? . . . Eh? . . . Oh! . . . *Ha!* . . . Hum!'

He was not really fooling, Felicity knew, and what he was told worried him. He moved a chair for her to sit down, but she knelt on the window seat looking at him. He listened for what seemed to be a long time, and then said: 'I didn't want to come up to Town, but if you really think it would help, I'll ask Fel if I may.' He grinned across at Felicity. 'Hm. All right, Tim—expect me about six o'clock, and ask Joan if she can put up with two extra for supper. . . . Call it dinner if you prefer, but we're provincials, remember.' He rang off, and looked more soberly at Felicity. He would have been very good-looking, but early in his youth he had suffered a broken nose when boxing; those were the days when plastic surgery had not been employed on such trivial matters. Now, this broadened his face and, especially when he smiled, gave him an expression of great good humour. He was a fair-haired man, and the fact that his hair was greying so that it now looked more flaxen than corn-coloured detracted nothing from his appearance. It was wiry, crinkly hair.

'Couldn't you have put it off?' Felicity asked. 'It looks as if it's going to keep fine, and we could have got all the grass cut.'

'You'd sit glued to the screen for Wimbledon,' Dawlish scoffed. 'Like to hear a funny story?'

'Or a fishy one?'

'Damn it, I did invite you as well,' protested Dawlish. He joined her at the window, sat down and stretched out his legs. Felicity handed him cigarettes from a box on a nearby table. 'Thanks, sweet. You've heard me talk about John Kelvedon, who——'

'I've remembered,' Felicity interrupted. 'He was killed in an air crash, wasn't he?'

'Yes. One of the best of the boys of the old brigade,' said Dawlish, who was often inclined to talk inanely and almost childishly when he was preoccupied; it made many people think that he was a fool, usually to their cost. 'Married one of the loveliest women imaginable, and I was one of the guard of honour.'

'I remember that, too,' Felicity said. 'He had one daughter, and his widow didn't marry again.'

Dawlish let smoke trickle out of the corner of his mouth. 'Right.'

'Who's in trouble?' inquired Felicity. 'The widow or her daughter?'

'Both.'

'Darling, I always try to be the patient and understanding wife, and I know that you were very fond of John Kelvedon, but it must be ten years since you met his widow. Is there really any reason why she should ask you to help because something's gone wrong?'

'Yes.'

'What?'

'She doesn't want to go to the police.'

'I think it's beginning to sound worse.'

'So far it only sounds peculiar,' said Dawlish. 'Mrs. K.

went to Cornwall for a fortnight's holiday, leaving the daughter in their flat in London. She's done that for week-ends often enough, but never for a whole two weeks. When she came back, the daughter had eloped.'

'Oh, no,' protested Felicity. 'You're surely not expected to go and chase after errant daughters!'

'No.'

'Pat, *must* you be so cryptic?'

'No,' said Dawlish, and took the cigarette from his lips and examined the end of it, as if it could explain life's major mysteries. Then he turned his cornflower blue eyes towards Felicity, crinkling them at the corners; when he looked at her like that, there was little she would refuse him. 'Sorry, sweet. The daughter, Gillian, left a note to say that she had run away with the most wonderful man in the world—don't scoff—and that she was going to be happy ever after, including a honeymoon touring France and a couple of weeks near Cannes. Naturally, it shook Mrs. K.'

'Did Gillian forget to get married?'

'According to Tim, who's been to the flat, the note was emphatic about the propriety of the situation,' said Dawlish, enunciating his words with great precision. 'The man's name was Macklin, and he told Gillian that he worked for Sharp and Company, a small firm of antique and art dealers.'

'And doesn't he?'

'Sharp, the owner of the business, says that he used to. Kay thinks there's something more in this than Sharp says. Sharp's given her a vague kind of description, but evades most of her questions. He's going away on business and she doesn't think it will be possible to get any more out of him—but he's made her more anxious than ever to find her daughter.' Dawlish tossed the cigarette out of the window. It fell among a bed of dahlias, already swollen with leaf and bud, and the smoke spiralled upwards in the rare sunlight. 'So far as Mrs. K. can trace, no one who knows her and her daughter has seen Gillian with Macklin. She had an idea that there was a man in the offing, but she didn't probe. Instead——'

'I really can't see why you should be drawn in,' Felicity said, rather glumly, 'but no doubt you will be. It's after four now, if you really want to get to Tim's by six we ought to have a cup of tea and then change.'

'Bless you,' said Dawlish. 'Yes. Debt to an old comrade in arms, so to speak. And you can understand why Mrs. K. doesn't want the police involved. Police lead to newspapers, she thinks, and——'

'She would hate any scandal,' Felicity completed for him. 'So would I! There's one good thing,' she added, standing up, 'this doesn't sound as if it will be dangerous.'

'If it did, I'd run a mile,' Dawlish declared, and tried to look as if he meant it. 'I'll bring the roto-scythe in while you're making tea. If we leave by half-past five——'

'If you want to get there by six we're going to leave at five sharp,' said Felicity. 'I'm not going to sit in terror all the way.'

'What a man you make me out to be,' said Dawlish.

'What a man you are,' Felicity retorted. 'I hope I didn't speak too soon.'

'About what?'

'About this not being dangerous.'

Dawlish grinned. 'The girl's probably got mixed up with a wrong 'un without knowing it, but before she makes a fuss Mrs. K. wants to make sure that it's necessary. She's going to be at Tim's just before six.'

'At least it will be a lovely drive,' Felicity said, and felt no greater sense of urgency than that.

. . . . .

Three hundred odd miles away, near the city of Fontainebleau, Gillian was sitting by Clive's side, watching his profile without thinking it odd that he seldom turned even to glance at her. It was a long, straight road. Poplars and silver birch made an avenue which sheltered them from the bright, hot sun, and the trunks of the trees cast black shadows on the road and continually shifting shadows over her and over Clive. It was very warm. The roof of the car was open, and the wind cut in about their heads. Gillian wore a large pair of sun-glasses with gilt rims, a present from him before they had left, three days ago.

He drove this car as if it were part of him and they belonged together. In the Paris traffic and on the open road he seemed to know exactly what was necessary to get the best performance while making the engine purr. That was one of the things about him which attracted her most; his great competence; there seemed nothing he could not do if he wanted it. Now, face set in repose, his strikingly handsome profile seemed to belong to someone else, to someone read about or seen on the screen; instead, they would soon be husband and wife.

Soon?

The first edge of doubt was in her mind, but she thrust it out. This was too perfect; he was too perfect. But they were to have been married in Paris. . . .

'As I'm part-time resident in France there's no real problem,' he had told her, 'but it's a little more difficult because you're not. Everything's in hand, though, and we shall be able to pick up the certificate when we get to Auxerre.'

That was only forty miles ahead.

Of course he wasn't deceiving her, she tried to persuade herself; then, with a part of her mind which seemed to persist, she asked: "But it *could* happen to me. Supposing it did? *Supposing it has!*" She kept staring at him, and the doubts grew stronger, threatening to rise up and choke her, as her happiness had on the night of the great decision. Well, supposing it had? She would have had four golden weeks. She would have had an experience denied to ninety-nine girls out of a hundred. This was the late twentieth century, and she belonged to it, had often boasted of belonging to it, laughing at outworn conventions.

Unexpectedly, Clive put his hand out and pressed her knee.

'Tired of driving, sweet?'

'It's lovely.'

'We have a day off tomorrow, remember. I have a man to see in Auxerre, as well as a certain engagement I don't want to break.'

Gillian's heart seemed to lift.

'Wonderful!'

Then Clive looked straight ahead at the unending ribbon of road, the tyres hummed on tar, the shadows of the trees zipped past them, *zp, zp, zp, zp, zp*, as if they were actually making a noise.

By now, Gillian knew, her mother would be home, and would have found the letter.

4

Gillian's Mother

'I LIKE HER,' Felicity thought, and as Mrs. Kelvedon was looking at Pat, Felicity had a chance to watch Pat, too: 'And so does he,' she decided. Then, she studied Mrs. Kelvedon, who was probably nearer fifty than forty, and very handsome; it was easy to imagine how striking she had been twenty years ago. She was running a little to fat; perhaps not really fat, Felicity decided, but probably she had to fight a constant battle against weight. She was dark, almost olive-skinned, with unusually bright and light blue eyes, strange in a dark-haired woman. Her hair was beginning to turn grey in the most becoming manner possible. It was a rich cluster of hair, such as few people had, and which Felicity greatly envied. She was wearing a linen suit, a little too tight for her; that was probably what gave the first impression.

' . . . I don't think you know Felicity,' Dawlish said. 'Fel, this is Kay Kelvedon.'

The two women murmured. Felicity felt that she was being quickly and shrewdly appraised, and felt again that she liked this woman, who smiled quite suddenly and warmly.

'It must be a terribly worrying time for you,' Felicity said.

'It is,' agreed Mrs. Kelvedon. 'It's extremely good of you both to come and see me. I honestly don't know whether I ought to go to the police or not. I'd much rather not.' She seemed to be summing Pat up, too, as she went on: 'It isn't simply a matter of scandal, I do assure you. If Gillian's really made a fool of herself with a man, a little scandal wouldn't do her any harm. It's an unhappy situation, but—well, I feel I want to try to make sure that I don't worsen it. If I could only find out whether the man really is a scoundrel, I would know whether it was worth while trying to find them and bring Gillian back without consulting the police.'

Felicity silently applauded.

'The trouble is, I've really no lead to give you,' Mrs. Kelvedon went on, and she smiled again; but beneath the smile there was the anxiety which showed in her eyes, in the tension at her lips, and in her body's tension, too. 'I simply know that she met this young man at a cocktail party given by Corrisons, one of the big antique dealers in London. Anyone with a trade card could get in, and'—she hesitated for a moment and then went on bitterly—'I couldn't go, and sent Gillian along to represent me.'

'Bad luck,' sympathized Dawlish. 'May I see her letter?'

'Of course.' Mrs. Kelvedon opened a large handbag, took a letter out, and handed it to him. 'She was very excited when she wrote it, obviously, and I don't think it will help at all.'

Dawlish read the letter quickly, and fully agreed with her. More than excitement showed between the lines; there was anxiety, a sense of guilt, a sense of distress at causing hurt; but there was the glowing description of the man Gillian had gone away with which told of a girl completely enthralled.

. . . and I simply can't describe or explain Clive. He's quite—wonderful. He is exactly what I always imagined my husband should be like. I am quite, quite, quite *sure that when you see him, you'll understand why I feel that it is so right.*

Forgive me, and pray for me, Mum darling,

Your Gill.

Dawlish handed the letter to Felicity, who noticed that as Dawlish had read it, Mrs. Kelvedon's eyes had misted over; but there was no sign of tears when Dawlish looked up, and said:

'You told Tim that you thought there was a man in the offing, didn't you?'

'Yes.'

'For how long?'

'Only a few days before I went away,' Mrs. Kelvedon answered.

'Didn't she say a word about him?'

'No.'

'Has she behaved in the same way before?'

'No, I wouldn't say so,' said Mrs. Kelvedon. She was sitting back in an armchair now, her ankles crossed. She had slim and very beautiful legs and small feet. 'Now and again she did when she was younger, but in the past two or three years she hasn't really been bowled over. The time was bound to come when she would be, I knew that; and I thought it had come.' Mrs. Kelvedon closed her eyes for a moment, and her face seemed suddenly cast into shadow. 'As apparently it had,' she added. 'I thought it would be folly to ask questions if Gillian wasn't ready to confide in me. I've always been very—very careful not to be too possessive. It's so easy when you've no one else.'

'I can imagine,' Felicity said.

'Can you remember when you first noticed this?' asked Dawlish.

'Very well. Gillian had come in late the night before, and I had an argument with myself about saying something to her or not. She was up late next morning, as often happened, and in a rush to get to the *salon*, so I didn't say anything. She was home fairly early that evening, but—well, she'd met him again by then.'

'So you only think she met him on the night of the cocktail party—you're not sure?'

'Not really sure, but there wasn't much doubt that she was excited about something the next morning, while rushing to get off to work.'

Dawlish said, 'Was she rushing to make sure you didn't notice anything?'

'I suppose it could be that.'

'Do you know what time the cocktail party ended?'

'Quite late—about half-past nine. But Gillian wasn't home until well after midnight. I suppose I should have made sure that I knew a little about it,' Mrs. Kelvedon went on, speaking very precisely, 'but it was simply a question of not wanting Gillian to think that I was trying to run her life for her. She always felt that she owed more to me than she really did—the truth is, Pat, we are really devoted.'

'Yes, I can see that,' said Dawlish, and went on quickly: 'Did she have any special girl friend?'

'No, not really. She knew the other models, of course, but I don't think she had any close friends.'

'Have you made any inquiries at her *salon*?'

'There hasn't really been time,' answered Mrs. Kelvedon. 'I didn't get back from my holiday until about lunchtime, you see—I stayed with friends in Blandford last night, and finished the journey this morning. The note was—well, quite a shock. The first thing I did was to telephone Sharp's. I know Sharp's quite well—in fact Mr. Sharp is an old friend. He was so non-committal that I immediately suspected that he had good reason to doubt this Macklin's integrity. I've already told you why I didn't—and still don't—want to go to the police, but I realized that I'd have to do something quickly, and called Tim. I was sure you would help if you were persuaded that it was a good cause, and I thought Tim could persuade you.'

'I'm persuaded,' Dawlish assured her, and his face lit up in a smile which seemed to ease Mrs. Kelvedon's anxiety. Then he went on: 'The quickest way to get results is to ask the police to help. I know them well enough to be sure they'll be discreet. Do you really mind if I get in touch with them?'

'I know it's absurd,' Mrs. Kelvedon said, 'but I'd much rather you didn't, unless—unless you have any reason to think that Gillian is in danger. Especially as Mr. Sharp is on his way to Paris—he thinks he might be able to find Macklin. But he might not, and I must do something. It's hard to explain why I feel so sure that if we set the police on to Gillian, she—well, we might spoil what's been a remarkably happy mother and daughter relationship. And——' she broke off.

Dawlish did nothing to prompt her, and she went on rather tensely, 'Gillian doesn't know yet, but I am thinking of getting married myself. I haven't told her that I have an understanding with a very old friend.' Exactly what did the word "friend" mean, Dawlish wondered? 'If this is just an elopement, you can imagine how Gillian would react to having the police question her. If this man makes a fool of her, she'll get over it sooner or later. But such dreadful things happen, and I feel that I must do something. I can't forget the story of that girl who went to France earlier this year thinking she was going to be married, and whose body was found in the mountains behind the Riviera. The Alpes Maritimes, aren't they? It's such a parallel in a way, isn't it?'

It would be easy for Dawlish to say, "Don't worry," or to try to put her off with platitudes. Felicity was glad that he did not.

'It won't be a parallel unless her body's found,' he said 'and that girl wasn't killed until she'd been in France for three weeks. I remember reading the case.'

Mrs. Kelvedon said in a strangled voice, 'Thank you.'

'I'll gladly see what I can do, and if it looks bad I'll ask the police to help discreetly,' Dawlish promised. 'Meanwhile I'll find out what I can about ferries to France.' He went to the telephone in a corner of this long, narrow room, overlooking a long narrow lawn surrounded by a herbaceous border superb with blooms and colour. Tim Beresford, who had sat on a couch during the whole of this without saying a word, heaved himself to his feet and said, 'How about tidying up, Kay?'

'I'd like to wait until I know what's going to happen next,' said Kay Kelvedon.

'I'll go and see if I can help Joan,' said Felicity. 'You

stay here, Tim.' She went out, sorry to have to leave, but knowing that Joan would have too much to do with three extra for dinner; and also knowing that with Joan even an emergency meal would be a banquet. Felicity went out, made her way to the old-fashioned kitchen where Joan looked a little hot but in no way flustered and was whipping cream for a gooseberry fool and raspberries. There was a spitting from the oven, and a bowl of batter with some filleted sole lay on a dish by the side of the gas stove.

'Start laying the table for me, there's a pet,' Joan said.

'What do you think's really happened to Gillian?' asked Felicity.

'I'm surprised that this has happened anyhow; I thought she had her head screwed on the right way,' Joan observed, practically. She finished whipping the cream, licked the fork and put it to one side. 'It's never so good without a bit of sugar,' she remarked. 'I don't know, Fel, except that she wouldn't have gone off like this unless she thought it was the real thing. If it weren't for that Ivy Marshall girl, I wouldn't think twice about it.'

. . . . .

'It's quaint and old-fashioned,' Clive said, as they stood by the window of the old hotel in the centre of Auxerre, looking out into a small church square filled with uneven cobbles which looked as if they had not seen rain for weeks. 'But I rather like the second-class French hotels, with their rickety chairs and the plumbing that won't plumb and the pipes which go squawk in the night, poor things. The floor boards always creak, too.' He put his weight on one, and it creaked; and Gillian found herself laughing. 'And the food will be absolutely first-class, I assure you.' He put the tips of his fingers and thumb together, and kissed them. 'The bed looks large enough for a family'—he was laughing at her—'and in the morning we shall be man and wife. I've spent half-an-hour trying to persuade the *M. le Maire* to marry us tonight, but there's some local rule against it. I had to hand over our passports and oil the waiting palm, but all's well. I'll bet you didn't expect to be married in Auxerre.'

'I'll bet I didn't,' Gillian said fervently; and the sunlight on the ancient tower of the church across the road was reflected in her radiant eyes; and suddenly the church clock began to strike the half-hour.

5

More Cause for Alarm

DAWLISH pulled into the courtyard at Scotland Yard, and was duly gratified by the greeting from two men on duty, one at the gates and one at the foot of the steps leading to the main building. He went upstairs briskly. At the top a sergeant saluted and gave him a knowing grin as he said:

'The Superintendent said it was all right to go straight in, Mr. Dawlish.'

'Thanks.'

'Got another job on the go?' the man asked.

Dawlish kept a straight face.

'You never know,' he said, and walked to the lift, which was a huge open cage, stepped in, and pressed the button so that it began to crawl slowly upwards. The speed of the lifts at the Yard were rather like its reputation: the wheels ground slowly, but they ground exceeding small; the lift travelled slowly, but it always arrived. At the landing, two large men were standing and waiting—and their faces brightened when they saw who it was.

'Hallo, Dawlish!'

'Come to set us all by the heels again?' asked the second man.

'As if I could, and as if I would even if I could,' Dawlish said.

'You certainly could and you probably would, and sometimes I think you should,' rejoined the man who had spoken first. 'Good night.'

'Good night,' Dawlish said, and strode on, yet heard the man speak to his companion quite clearly.

'A pity he turned down the Assistant Commissioner's job. He'd have made things hum.'

'Think he was really offered it?'

'Positive.'

Dawlish was smiling, a little tight-lipped. For the post of Assistant Commissioner of the Criminal Investigation Department had in fact been offered to him, to the disgust of some and the delight of many: and there were times when he wished profoundly that he had accepted. To feel that he was the leader of this almost fantastic organization would have done something to his ego which was never likely to be done now. His grin broadened. If he were offered the job again tomorrow he would still turn it down, and there was always the great satisfaction of knowing that after years of clashing with the police and years in Military Intelligence, he was regarded as a sufficiently sober citizen to be offered the post. Bill Trivett, whom he was going to see, had once said that he was a "natural" detective.

That was a comforting thought, too, and the kind of thing which Tim Beresford and Felicity were probably now saying to Kay Kelvedon; but she would not easily be reassured. She was quite a woman, and she had a mind of her own. How many mothers, in like circumstances, would have been so definite about keeping away from the police?

He had not told her he was coming here, and would not tell her, unless there was a sudden emergency or some deeper cause for fear.

He wondered what Gillian was like as a person. He knew what she looked like, for several photographs were in his pocket, but a shapely figure had nothing to do with temperament and with strength of character.

He came to a door marked: "Supt. Trivett," tapped and opened the door on Trivett's 'Come in.' Trivett was standing by the window, his head and shoulders outlined against the brightness of the early evening sky. The sun was shining on the Thames and turning it to gold. The gay awnings of the big pleasure boats seemed twice as colourful as on a drab evening, and there seemed a promise of settled weather at last. Dawlish did not give a thought to the weather as he shook hands.

Trivett was obviously really pleased to see him.

Dawlish had not met him for several months, and seeing Bill Trivett usually had a salutary effect. It had now. Trivett was a good-looking man and exactly the same age as Dawlish; and he was always immaculately dressed. When Dawlish had first met him, his hair had been jet black; now it was silvery, and it curled slightly at the temples in a rather old-world way, as if Trivett was establishing his right of a Scotland Yard detective to have a character of his own. For a moment Dawlish almost felt his age, and for a moment the middle forties seemed old.

'Sit down,' Trivett said, and asked about Felicity and Beresford, reported on his own wife, Grace, and then pushed a carved wooden box of cigarettes across his polished desk, which was almost clear of papers.

'Care for a whisky?' he asked.

'Thanks,' said Dawlish, and as Trivett bent down to take bottle, syphon and glasses out of a cupboard in his desk, he went on, 'Do you know an antique dealer named Sharp?'

'In Pottle's Row?'

'That's the chap.'

'Yes, I know of him,' Trivett said.

'What's his business and reputation like?'

'Small, exclusive, good,' answered Trivett. 'It's really a one-man show, but he employs a few men on commission, and buys on commission, too. Don't tell me you're going into the antique business.'

'No,' said Dawlish. He took his drink. 'Thanks. Perdition to all criminals.' He drank. 'Be patient for five minutes, will you?' he pleaded, and then told Trivett everything he knew, taking out the photographs as he finished, and placing them one by one in front of the Yard man. First, a face only, in profile; Gillian had quite a profile. Then a full face; and there was a hint of laughter in that, enough to suggest that she might take after her mother. Next there was a silhouette, side view.

'Nice statistics,' Trivett observed. 'Quite a shape, too.'

'Try this,' said Dawlish, and handed him a photograph of Gillian standing in a close-fitting dress and looking as if she had eyes only for him. 'All that, but no money—not to say money.'

'How much?'

'Seven or eight hundred a year from her job. The mother makes about twice as much as the owner of a small antique and bric-a-brac shop.'

'Hmm,' said Trivett. 'And there's no description of Macklin at all?'

'Nothing,' Dawlish answered. 'I've been round to his office, but there's only a part-time secretary on duty and she doesn't seem to know much. Sharp himself has gone to Paris. But if Macklin is dangerous I wouldn't like to stand by doing nothing until we can contact Sharp. How long would it take you to make sure that the girl did go to France?'

'Forty-eight hours,' Trivett answered.

'I mean in this modern age of speed.'

'We don't keep a record these days,' Trivett explained. 'The French do, and the passport should be stamped, but that's all. I could telephone Calais and the other French Channel ports, but we might have to include Belgium and Holland, and it would take a long time. I can have a word with our chap who handles most of the jobs at the coast, and with Mick. He could send a full report in by tomorrow.'

'Try, will you?' urged Dawlish. 'If we can find someone who remembers the girl, too, we might get a description of the man.'

'You're slipping,' Trivett said.

'Eh?'

'This is the end of June, remember. The cross-channel traffic is nearing its peak. I daresay five thousand people go through every port every day. The chance of anyone remembering even a girl with a face and figure like this is pretty slim. The best chance is if she went to Calais; we had a special watch kept at Calais in the last week or so, old Fred Maxim was there. Wonder if Fred's still in his office,' Trivett added as an afterthought, and lifted a telephone. 'See if Mr. Maxim's in, will you?' He held on. 'Knowing you, it wouldn't surprise me if you had some luck right away. I—oh, Fred, working overtime? . . . Can't spare a minute to see an old enemy of ours, can you? . . . Pat Dawlish.' He chuckled. 'Fine.' He rang off. 'For some odd reason, he would like to see you.'

'There were always some nice people at the Yard,' Dawlish riposted. 'Bill—how far did you get on the Ivy Marshall job?'

'So that's on your mind, is it?'

'Almost a parallel,' Dawlish reminded him. 'She left home without warning, said she was going to get married, disappeared—and was found dead a few weeks later. She was an attractive girl, too, and she was an assistant in an antique shop. I wish Mrs. Kelvedon didn't know how she had been killed.'

Trivett said, 'It wasn't pleasant.' He rubbed his chin, and the room was so quiet that the sound of rasping actually reached Dawlish's ears; and then a tug hooted on the river. 'We didn't get very far, but we have a long list of people who knew Ivy Marshall, and the first thing I'll do is find out if anyone knew her also knew Gillian Kelvedon.'

'Thanks.'

The door swung open on Dawlish's words, and a lanky man with a long nose, and who was nearly bald, came in grinning. He had bony hands and a powerful grip, and he picked up the glass which Trivett had ready for him almost like a conjuror. 'Cheers,' he said, and drank. 'What bad news have you brought, Mr. Dawlish?'

'A job which is rather like the Ivy Marshall one,' Trivett said.

The grin faded from Maxim's face, and there was a dark look in his eyes. He hesitated before saying:

'I hope it isn't a rubber stamp of it.' He drank again, and put down his glass. 'No more, thanks. Why pick on me?'

'Remember your job at Calais?'

'Stop being funny.'

'Just testing your memory,' Trivett said. 'Did you see this girl?' He held out the profile and the full face. Dawlish watched the way Maxim's eyes narrowed, as if he had suddenly switched on concentration; and he saw how keen those eyes were. Maxim had a memory for faces which was second to none at the Yard, and whenever a special look-out was required at ports or airfields for wanted people who might be travelling under assumed names, and disguised, he had the job; at Calais recently he had been looking for a wife murderer whom he had spotted on the last day of a week's vigil.

He picked up the photograph, and then looked straightly at Dawlish.

'Yes,' he answered.

Dawlish just stopped himself from saying, 'Sure?' and asked quietly:

'You can't perform another miracle, can you, and remember who she was with?'

'Yes,' answered Maxim.

'I knew it,' said Trivett, and raised his hands in a token of surrender. 'If it's luck you need, it's Dawlish who'll get it. Sure, Fred?'

'Don't be silly,' Maxim retorted. 'That girl would stick out a mile.' His grin flashed. 'In more ways than one! She was with a fair-haired chap, tallish, one of these film-star types—in fact I remember thinking that it was Tod Benson at first, but it wasn't. Same kind of fair hair, a kind of full jaw and lips. The girl looked on top of the world, and I remember thinking that I hoped she'd got her marriage lines all safely tucked away.'

'He looked like that, did he?' Trivett asked.

'As far as a man can,' said Maxim, and grinned again. 'Hark at us—talking like a couple of bishops. Gimme another, Bill, will you? I obviously need a pick-me-up.'

'What ferry did they take?' Trivett asked.

'The *Lord Warden*. I think it was the early morning one,

I remember thinking that anyone who could look as fresh as that girl did at that hour of the morning must be really something in the evening. Good job I've got a memory.'

He took his second whisky, raised his glass to Trivett, and drank again. 'Cheers. Well, I hope she isn't going to be another Ivy Marshall. I never was in favour of burying people alive.' The way he said it sent a shiver through Dawlish, and obviously it affected Trivett, too: there was something hideous about the possibility that the girl whose photographs they had studied might possibly suffer the fate of Ivy Marshall.

'Well, I'll get cracking,' Trivett promised Dawlish. 'I'll keep it quiet, just find out who was at that cocktail party, and find out all I can about Clive Macklin, who's like Tod Benson—that's a big help, Fred, thanks—I'll call you as soon as I can. All right, Pat?'

'Thanks.' Dawlish didn't move, and both of the others watched him intently, guessing that he was thinking fast; guessing that he might show once again his remarkable faculty of side-stepping most of the normal processes of logic and arriving at a conclusion a long way ahead of most people. The fact that he was occasionally wrong simply made him human. 'Bill, could you arrange for me to have a look at details of the cars which went over on that ferry, and to talk to our customs chaps at Dover? If this couple were so noticeable, we might pick something up quickly. I can use the likeness to Benson, too. You could telephone me at Dover or at Calais, couldn't you?'

'What do you stand to gain?' asked Trivett.

'I might be able to pick the trail up from Calais and start trailing them,' Dawlish said. 'If we can identify the car and get a photograph of Benson I might gain twenty-four hours. That wouldn't do any harm.'

'You'd have to do it off your own bat,' Trivett told him. 'Until we can definitely say that this girl is missing or in danger, we can't expect any co-operation from the French police.'

'I'll risk it,' Dawlish said. 'Can't remember anything else about this chap, Fred, can you?'

'As a matter of fact, I can,' Maxim told him, not without pride. 'I heard him talking to the French customs people in fluent French while they cleared his car. Not much of a formality these days.' He raised a finger and shook it reprovingly. 'Wait for it. The car was a Jaguar sports, one of these black all-weather jobs. They cut quite a dash in it.'

'Now all we need to know is what road they took,' Dawlish said.

6

Ceremony

CLIVE lay sleeping.

Gillian, with a strange mixture of excitement, ecstasy and guilt, watched him for several minutes, and was sorely tempted to wake him, but he seemed to be heavily asleep, so she did not. His fair hair bristled on his chin, and she had never seen a man, close to, who needed a shave. For that matter, she had never done a great many of the things which she had in the past three days.

She heard the church clock strike.

She pushed back the single blanket, all she had needed for the night, and that only after Clive had gone to sleep, and tiptoed to the window. A board creaked, the board he had demonstrated on the previous evening. The window was ajar, and she could see a shaft of sunlight striking a red brick building opposite: the market place, Clive had told her. He seemed to know the road and the places as well as he knew London, and she was quite sure about one thing: when he had said that the food was good, he had been right. "Exquisite" was almost the only word for the meal in the strangely modern dining-room downstairs; "perfect" the only word for the soft-footed waitresses. The proprietor had come and spoken to Clive, obviously as an old acquaintance, and they had talked freely in French.

Gillian had never realized how little French she knew.

She hugged a wrap round her shoulders and reached the window without making the boards creak again. Outside, the town seemed to be waking up. Two old people and a young boy, all looking like peasants, were unloading a handcart which was piled high with cauliflowers, string sacks of peas and carrots, and small onions. Two big trucks were being unloaded by the entrance to the market itself. A dozen people were strolling about as if aimlessly, and a dilapidated old car trundled up the steep, cobbled approach to the market; its engine seemed to splutter and fade before it reached its rightful spot. Two old men and a young girl, raven haired, fresh-faced and quite strikingly beautiful, climbed out and began to unload the vegetables without attempting to move the car.

It was fascinating.

Nothing *could* go wrong, surely.

Gillian turned, and looked at Clive, who had not stirred. He hadn't put on pyjamas, and the sheet was down so that his chest was bare. He was powerful and his flesh was firm but free from blemish, and it was tanned a light brown, as if he had already been in the sun a lot this year.

She went across, stood by the bed and stared at him—and quite suddenly he darted his hands towards her and caught her, and drew her down. His lips crushed against hers and she was breathless, but there was nothing she could do to free herself until he let her go.

When he did, she was lying by his side, and his eyes were laughing at her.

'Can't you sleep?'

'How long'—she had to pause for breath—'how long had you been watching me?'

'Five minutes. I wish it had lasted a lot longer.'

'It can last as long as you like,' Gillian said.

'Then, by God, it's going to last a long time!' Clive said fiercely, and kissed her again. . . .

They had breakfast at a small table overlooking the market, which had become a seething mass of people who had arrived in brand new vans and old cars which hardly seemed to hold together, in horse-drawn carts and donkey-drawn carts and who had walked, cycled, or come on motor-scooters—all having only one thing in common: merchandise to sell. Eggs and butter, cream and milk, cheese and vegetables, fruit and meat, fish and fowl—so much was carried into the market hall that it seemed as if it would burst its sides. People kept streaming into it, but few seemed to come out.

The *croissants* were light and appetising, the butter creamy, and there was luscious cherry jam.

'Now,' said Clive, 'you have to make up really specially today; this is to be quite an occasion. I'll nudge you when you have to say yes—there's no need to say no! You needn't be the slightest bit embarrassed because you don't know the language. It's a very simple civil ceremony here, nearly everyone gets married again in church, of course. Sure you don't mind the civil ceremony?'

'Mind!' Gillian echoed.

But she wished that she could understand the language. . . .

M. le Maire was a short, pale-faced man with a clipped black beard, and looked a little like she imagined a young Jewish rabbi to be. He was dressed in a dark-grey clerical suit and wore a bright crimson bow tie, which was not only lurid but a little ludicrous. Words rippled off his tongue, and his eyes flashed. A middle-aged woman was witness, and an old man who seemed to serve no purpose at all. From first to last, the ceremony in a small house near the market took less than ten minutes.

'Now all you have to do is sign the book,' Clive said. 'Use your maiden name this time—you start signing as Mrs. Macklin after this.'

It was just an old, black-bound book, with entries in it rather like the entries on birth and marriage certificates, and Gillian could not properly understand the writing, although she could make out her own name. She signed; and for some unaccountable reason she shivered, although it was very warm in here. The bearded man shook hands; at least she understood when he said "*Adieu,*" and partly understood when he was wishing them well. When the door closed on him, Gillian realized that he had not once smiled.

Clive's fingers were firm upon her arm as they walked away. She felt strangely subdued, almost as if this were a kind of anti-climax. Neither of them spoke as they reached the narrow lane which led to their hotel, with the market at one side. The babble of voices from the crowd was made worse every now and again by the crowing of a cockerel or the clucking of a hen.

'We stay here all day today and leave early tomorrow morning, sweetheart,' Clive said.

'Yes,' Gillian agreed.

'Just as well we'd allowed a day free for a real honeymoon!' Clive said, 'I have to take the car to a garage—there's a place on the outskirts of the town where they specialize in English cars. I wasn't satisfied with the engine last night, and we don't want a breakdown.'

'If we could break down here for a month I'd love it.'

'But the real holiday starts at Cannes!' Clive reminded her. They reached the hotel and went upstairs to their room; strangely, Gillian felt a greater sense of shyness and of wonder now than she had when they had come here last night. The sense of guilt was gone, too. She kept thinking of her mother, and yet did not want to talk of her to Clive: it would look as if she had some regrets. She could send a card tomorrow; she must not do anything at all which might even bring a faint cloud to this bright day.

. . . . .

They drove to the garage soon afterwards, left the Jaguar with a boy who looked too young to know the difference between a plug and a carburettor, and hired an old Renault which clattered and rattled and yet which went at surprising speed. As it shook them about it made them laugh helplessly; every bump in the road, every swerve round a bend on the by-roads, every time a farm cart or a team of horses came towards them, they laughed. It was a kind of furious gaiety, partly due to relief, and they were laughing when, a little after six o'clock, they returned to the garage where the young boy was bending over a motor-cycle which looked as if it had been buried for years, and recently dug up.

Clive waved to him as he got out. Gillian followed him,

wishing more than ever that she knew more French and telling herself that she would have to persuade Clive to teach her.

Then, she saw him frown.

The quiet Frenchman began to wave his arms about. Their voices rose. For a minute, Gillian thought that they would come to blows, but suddenly they quietened down and Clive forced a smile, then turned away towards her. She could tell that he was really upset.

'He's sent the distributor head away for replacement, as he hasn't any spares here,' he told her. 'It will be three days before he gets it back! We can't possibly wait. We'll have to carry on in this old wreck of a Renault until I can pick up a better car on the road.'

'Oh, this one's good enough, darling!'

'That's where we don't agree,' said Clive gruffly. 'I don't like the idea of my wife being thrown about as if she were on a roller coaster, and tomorrow we ought to get a move on; we can't crawl round like we've been doing today. In any case only the best is good enough for my wife! But the worst blow of all was really to my pride.'

Gillian said, 'How?'

'The little blighter said that he thought I said we'd be here for three or four days—which means that he says he didn't understand my French!'

Gillian found herself laughing.

They both laughed hilariously, and the little Frenchman, who looked too young, beamed broadly and waved to them as they went back to their hotel.

. . . . .

About the same time that day, Dawlish finished talking to a British Railways representative at Calais, after a long session with customs officials and port authorities. He had a photograph of Tod Benson with him, and every other man who saw the photograph "recognized" him, but none could have said for certain what day he had passed through the port. Two women officials smiled brightly when they saw the photograph and were quite sure that they had seen him, and most of the people also remembered Gillian; only the men could identify her from the photograph. Dawlish strolled into the office of the Automobile Association. There one young man in khaki serge looked far too hot, and a middle-aged man in the blue serge of the Royal Automobile Club looked even hotter. But they brightened up when they saw Dawlish, and the young man offered limp-looking cigarettes from a pale blue packet.

'How did you get on, Mr. Dawlish?'

'Not much doubt that we've got the right car,' Dawlish said. 'All we want now is to make sure which road they took.'

'I can't believe that a couple like that wouldn't look in on Paris,' remarked the young man.

'You're probably right,' agreed Dawlish. 'How many Jaguar service stations are there on the road to Paris?'

'Well—not many.'

'Think you could find out the authorised dealers for me?' asked Dawlish. 'Jaguar dealers are more likely to notice Jags than anyone else, and that one stood out.'

'I'm sure the Head Office would want us to help,' the A.A. man said. 'We'll telephone and ask them for a complete list of Jaguar agents in France. It should be here by the morning.'

'Fine,' said Dawlish, and glanced at the telephone. He had been here all day, and had hoped that there would be a message from Trivett, but none had yet come.

The French cigarette had a harsh taste, and he wished he had not accepted it, but smoked a little for appearances sake. As he stubbed it out, the telephone bell rang.

'A.A. office,' the older man answered. 'Oh, yes, he's here. For you Mr. Dawlish.' He held out the receiver, and then he and his companion went out, leaving Dawlish in full possession. This would be Trivett, surely, with news of a kind.

'Dawlish speaking,' he announced.

'*Good* evening, Mr. Dawlish,' said Felicity.

'Fel! What a sound for tired ears!' Dawlish relaxed

immediately, and put one foot on the edge of a small desk. 'How are you, and how——'

'Bill Trivett just telephoned and I said I'd call you instead of letting him,' Felicity said. 'Apparently Sharp is still away, but Macklin is known to Corrisons. He's what the Trade calls a high-class runner or contact man,' Felicity went on. 'He knows a lot about antiques and *objets d'art*, and travels all over Europe examining pieces which can be bought at low prices, and recommending them to different dealers. Corrisons have bought through him occasionally, but recently he's been on a retainer for Sharp's. He's had a working permit for France for years, and is as fluent in French as in English!'

'Hmm,' said Dawlish, and put the other foot up to join the first. 'Has he a record?'

'Bill says no, neither here nor in Paris. Bill's checked with the Sûreté.'

'Trust our William,' Dawlish said. 'Anything else, sweet?'

'No, not really,' Felicity replied. 'There's no record of Macklin's address in the records at Sharp's, and the police haven't yet traced him or his car.'

'It's the nearest thing to certain that I know the car and its number—a London registration,' Dawlish said, 'but the problem is going to be tracing it over here. If Macklin hasn't a record Bill can't do much, so we can't expect the police to help unless there's a complaint from Sharp about the missing goods. Darling, do you think that you——'

'I think that I could pack our clothes for two weeks, and be on the first ferry tomorrow morning,' Felicity told him. 'But if that isn't what you want . . .'

Dawlish was grinning happily.

'You took the very words out of my mouth, sweetheart! Two weeks in France that we didn't expect—what could be better? There's one thing you could bring over—a list of Jaguar agents in France and on the Continent. I think you might find that Tim has one for that old Jag of his, and if he hasn't, you'd better ask Lawley's in Haslemere, they'll have one up their sleeves. Bring as many pound notes as you can; we'll have to change 'em on this side of the Channel. They aren't very strict these days, I doubt if anyone will even ask you how much English money you've got. All right?'

'Yes. Pat . . .'

'Yes?'

'Mrs. Kelvedon would obviously like to come with me. I was talking to her on the telephone, and she says that she can arrange to shut the shop. What do you think?'

'Persuade her that it will make things infinitely more difficult—booking rooms at hotels, that kind of thing,' urged Dawlish. 'And tell her that I always work better when I'm on my own. I'd much rather not have her with us.'

'I'll see what I can do,' Felicity promised. 'Have you got a hotel for the night?'

'Quite near the ferry; I'll be waiting for you,' Dawlish said. 'And don't come without that Jaguar list; I can't wait to get after Macklin's car.'

7

Message

It was bright sunlight when Clive Macklin woke, although it was only six o'clock in the morning. He heard a single motor-scooter in the distance, but it did not come nearer; doubtless it was that which had woken him. He turned to look at Gillian, and there was tautness at his lips and a shadow in his eyes as he did so. She was very lovely, and the abandon of sleep seemed to make her even younger than she was. That cluster of dark hair seemed almost blue-black against the white pillow. Her shoulders were bare, and she had pulled up a single blanket; it was a little more chilly this morning. Macklin eased himself up on one elbow, looking down at her; then he got out of bed and went into the little bathroom leading off the bedroom. He made as little noise as possible, washed and shaved and, by twenty-past six, was back in the bedroom dressing. Gillian had not moved. It must have been two o'clock before they had settled for sleep.

He kept thinking about Andrew Sharp and the threat he had made. It was an awful situation to be in a man's grasp so tightly. He hadn't meant to kill Ivy Marshall, and still shuddered at the recollection, but she had meant nothing to him as a girl—as a woman.

But Gillian. . . .

He hadn't realized that anyone could mean so much.

Nothing must happen to her, but—had Sharp told the truth? Would he be satisfied if Gillian were out of England for three weeks? Was it possible that for some reason he needed her dead, and intended to make him, Clive Macklin, kill her?

He wouldn't; he would defy the devil!

After a few minutes an icy thought came. He was in Sharp's hands, and if it really came to a question of his life or Gillian's . . .

Macklin tried not to think about that any more. There was no certainty about it, and Sharp might be fully satisfied if Gillian were kept in France for a few weeks.

He crept to the door, and the very last step made a board creak so loudly that he thought it was bound to wake Gillian, but it did not.

He went out.

A young girl dressed in black and wearing black stockings and red shoes was polishing the floor at the landing, and she gave him a soft and shy '*Bonjour!*' He smiled at her; he had always found it easy to smile at young girls. He went down the wooden staircase, careful on the polished boards. A big bright chromium urn was hissing and bubbling slightly. A dozen tables were laid for breakfast with red tablecloths, and a huge basket of *croissants* and a smaller one of *petit pains* stood on a table by a large jug of milk, and butter which was floating in icy water.

He went out.

The old Renault was parked almost opposite the front door, but he did not go towards it. He went instead to the centre of the town, passing a newspaper shop which was already open, and a bakery from which the smell of new bread was rich and warm. A woman in white was stacking great long crusty loaves in racks as he passed. This was on a corner, and he turned it, and a few yards along stopped at a dark, gloomy shop window. On show was some old furniture, a small gilt mirror, and a few glass oddments, but at the back French furniture of several periods was jumbled together. He tried the handle of the door, and when it did not open, pressed a bell which made a noisy sound on the other side of the door. He lit an English cigarette, stood waiting, and was about to press the bell again when he heard footsteps inside; a door at the back of the shop opened and a middle-aged man came forward. He was wearing an old blue shirt and a pair of trousers held up at the waist by a tie. His big head was tousled, and his fleshy lips were parted, so that his teeth showed, and he hadn't shaved for days. He scowled as he unbolted the door and turned the key, scowled more deeply when he stood to one side.

'So it is you again,' he said.

'Why must you always say the obvious, Flambon?' asked Clive irritably. 'Is there a message for me?'

'I don't know. I will go and see.'

'You mean there is one,' Macklin said tartly. 'You have to make it difficult.'

'You have to come at this hour of the morning?'

'Supposing we stop arguing?' Macklin growled. He stood in the shop, looking round at the dusty furniture as the man Flambon went through the back again. His shuffling footsteps sounded clearly. Macklin caught sight of a small table in one corner. He went across to it and found that one leg was missing, which made it of very little value as it was. He was examining it in the light of the window, when Flambon came back carrying a letter.

'That table is worth a hundred thousand francs,' he said. 'Tomorrow I shall have it repaired.'

'Next year, you mean,' Macklin said. 'I might recommend fifteen thousand francs.'

'It is no time of the morning to joke, *m'sieu.*'

'Don't tell me you ever joke!' Macklin took a five-hundred franc note from his pocket, handed it to the other, won a reluctant *merci*, and then went out, without opening the letter. He slipped this into his pocket and walked moodily back towards the window. As he turned into the street he saw Gillian at the window, just as she had been yesterday when he had seen her back view. The wrap was round her shoulders, and she was watching the now empty market and a few people struggling into the big hall. Obviously she was not aware of being watched, and she looked—ravishing.

Then she turned and saw him. Her face lit up as she waved. He smiled and waved back, kissed his hand to her, and saw her turn away. She would expect him to go straight upstairs, and he would have preferred a few minutes on his own; the way she had looked had made his heart thump with an unfamiliar vigour. He did not walk quickly, and waited until he reached the hotel before taking out the letter and opening it.

It was a typewritten note, headed Paris, and it said:

"You will visit Bourges next, please."

There was a scrawled signature which it would be impossible to read, unless one had a clue, that this had been signed by Sharp. So he was in France.

'I suppose it could be worse,' Macklin said aloud. He pushed the letter back into his pocket and hurried up the twisting stairs. The little girl with the red shoes was carrying a tray with coffee, *croissants* and butter on it, and she stood aside for him to pass.

'*Petit dejeuner pour vous, m'sieu?*'

'*Pour deux personnes, avec beaucoup de beurre et beaucoup de confiture.*'

'*Oui, m'sieu!*'

'*Café tres chaude, si'l vous plaît,*' Macklin said, and passed her to his room. He opened the door and saw Gillian dressed in a sleeveless cotton frock with huge green flowers on a white background, and off one shoulder. He actually stood still, startled by the very look of her, by the sense of wonderment that he had not known for many years.

And suddenly, by her side, there appeared the image of another girl, standing by her, smiling, a good-looking girl although not like Gillian.

Ivy.

Ivy Marshall. . . .

The vision faded.

Gillian said, as if startled, 'Clive! What's the matter?'

'Matter?'

'You looked—scared.'

'Good lord, am I likely to be scared of you?' asked

Macklin, and he forced a laugh which did not sound natural. 'I knew you were lovely, but not *so* lovely. That dress is superb.'

The puzzlement faded from Gillian's eyes and she pirouetted round.

'Like it?'

'I like anything that does the impossible, and the dress makes you look even better.'

'Sweetheart, you say the nicest things,' Gillian said lightly, and she turned away and went to the window. He thought that she went more quickly than she had intended, as if her mood had changed. She stood looking out, and there was now the beauty of the curve of her waist to her hips, of her long thighs, and the gentle curve of her legs down to perfect ankles for him to see. But he hardly noticed them. His heart began to beat a little faster again, not because of her beauty, but because of the way she had turned round—as if she did not want to meet his eye. What could he have said to make her do that? Had he been too glib?'

That was always the danger; he had said things like this so often that they came too easily.

He remembered the first time he had seen a change in Ivy Marshall's expression—when she had begun to suspect the truth about him. That was when it had become inevitable that she should be murdered. And with these hands, which now touched Gillian, he had suffocated her and buried her—not knowing she was still alive. He had had no feeling for her, remember, and he loved Gillian. She would never know that she owed her life to him.

Sharp would undoubtedly have killed her had she stayed in England. Macklin wondered why, but did not dwell on it. His hands rested lightly on the satiny beauty of Gillian's skin, close to her neck. He had stolen up on the other girl, from behind, and had swung round, exclaiming. 'Don't touch me!'

Gillian swung round.

Her eyes were misty as if with tears, and there was something in her expression which he did not understand, but it was not suspicion, thank God! She clung to him. He could feel the throb of her heart and the pressure of her body against him.

'Darling, what is it?' he asked, bewildered. 'What's the matter? What have I done?'

'Nothing,' she said in a muffled voice. 'Nothing, Clive, I—it's just that I'm so happy.'

'What a way to show it!'

'I know. I'm silly.'

'Stay like that,' urged Clive Macklin. 'Don't ever change.' They were quiet for a moment, and then there came a rattle of cups and saucers. He turned away from her and went across to the door, while she moved the table in front of the window, so that they could look out.

The girl in the red shoes came in smiling and bobbing, set everything out, and pointed to a huge mountain of butter and two dishes of the cherry jam. There was a quick patter of French, and she went out, obviously delighted.

'When I can speak French like you I shall feel satisfied,' Gillian said. 'I don't know what's the matter with me, it must be marriage—but I'm famished!'

'I saw that yesterday, that's why I ordered plenty of everything,' Macklin said. 'And you'll need a good start; we've a long drive today. I've had a change of instructions.'

'Where to, darling?'

'Bourges,' he told her. 'It's a big place, several hundred miles away, very charming when we get to it, but a pretty boring run. How we're going to regret the Jag.' He was sitting down, and pouring out the coffee. 'We won't be able to make it in one day, though.'

'I don't mind how long we take,' Gillian said, 'but how did you get a message?'

'I have to leave my places of call in London and they write or send a telegram to shops where I'll be calling. That way I can change hotels if I want to,' he explained. 'After

Bourges we probably go to Digne, that's in the Alpes Maritimes. And then——'

'Cannes!'

'Cannes and the bright blue sea,' Clive promised her, and looked away abruptly, for he thought, "If we ever get there." If Sharp meant to kill her, he *might* intend to use him, Clive, to do it; might plan to blackmail him into murdering the girl he loved, or . . .

He did not let himself finish the thought.

8

Luck?

'HERE we go again,' said Dawlish. 'This time we might have some luck. If we can't trace the car this side of Paris we're going to have trouble. Paris is littered with Jag agencies.'

'I'm afraid it's going to be a wild goose chase,' Felicity said.

'Could be,' admitted Dawlish. 'Wish we hadn't come?'

'If it weren't for everything I remember about Ivy Marshall I would be sorry that we had to worry about anything,' Felicity said. 'I read all about the case the night before I left.'

'So I guessed.'

'And this Kelvedon girl . . .'

'Yes?'

'She looks . . .'

'I'll say it for you. Good.'

'I suppose that's the word,' Felicity agreed slowly. 'Pat, isn't there any way in which we can get the French police to help us? Surely they would be able to trace a car without a lot of trouble.'

'They could,' Dawlish agreed in turn, 'but it's difficult enough to get full co-operation from the police even at home, and it's worse here, there are so many different authorities. The people in the Seine province are almost foreigners to those in the Rhone or the Loire, and it would take a major murder to get them all clicking at the same time. After all,' Dawlish went on, 'why should they? A pretty young woman of full age has eloped. *C'est l'amour*. Shrug, shrug. If Bill Trivett gets the slightest indication that this might be tied up with the Marshall murder, or if Sharp reports the theft, he'll pull every string he can—and he'll advise us, too. I send him a telegram saying where we'll be each night, so that he can contact us without any delay. We just plod on.'

'I suppose so,' Felicity said.

They were driving along a narrower road than many in France, and Dawlish was watching the bends as they went through a range of low hills. Thanks to Felicity, he was at the wheel of his pet, a Lagonda with a special body and an engine which would do everything ever asked of it. It was purring softly, although they had already driven over two hundred miles in the past four hours and had made stops at three towns. Just ahead lay the Forest of Fontainebleau, and once they were on the road leading to the town itself he could give the car its head. It looked very cool among the trees, and scorching hot on the road and in the car itself, but heat seldom worried Felicity, and she looked as fresh and cool in a lemon-coloured sun dress, her shoulders bare, and little jacket hanging on the back of her seat. She wore a wide-brimmed hat of exactly the same shade of yellow, and it shaded her face from the discomfort of direct sunshine.

They reached the straight road through the forest, and five minutes later turned off into the town. By accident Dawlish found himself slowing down outside the palace. At least a dozen motor-coaches were standing in the great square outside it, and there were hundreds of cars. Every other person in sight was carrying a camera, and it seemed to Dawlish that the click-click-click of them was like the noise of crickets.

'Would you like to go and have a look at the carp and the lake while I find the agency?' he suggested.

'No, it isn't fair to——'

'Nonsense,' Dawlish said, and glanced in his mirror, then opened the door and got out. He opened Felicity's door for her, handed her down and said, 'You've plenty of loose money, haven't you?'

'Yes. Pat, are you sure you won't mind?'

'Let's meet at the car in an hour,' Dawlish said. He

pressed her hand, watched her as she turned into the gates of the palace, and then turned towards the right, where one could enter the grounds without having to go through the palace itself. She walked gracefully and rather slowly, almost purring in the afternoon sun. Dawlish wiped the sweat off his forehead, got back into the car, and drove towards the main part of the town. He found a parking place, locked the car, and strolled towards the large garage with Shell pumps outside it. When he reached it he turned round casually and looked along the way he had come.

He saw what he expected to see: a little Volkswagon with a Paris number plate. It was a pale grey car, the kind which could almost go into the boot of the Lagonda. It slowed down near the Lagonda, as if the driver were looking for a parking place, but there was plenty of room, and the driver need do no more than drive in.

Dawlish stepped past the petrol pumps. The huge glass door of the showroom was open, to show gleaming new cars beyond, but no one was in sight. He stepped into it, saw a door at the far end, and went through this. A moment later he stepped into the street nearer his car, and saw the Volkswagon drawn up close to it. A man was walking round the car and trying the handles. He was youthful-looking, with a round head and close-cut hair, and he wore a pale-coloured linen suit. Dawlish did not interfere, but studied the driver of the car, a man who looked little more than a boy.

The first man gave up.

The driver called out in a voice which Dawlish could just hear:

'It is dangerous. Come away.'

'But it is important.'

'It must wait until after dark.'

'I tell you it is important,' insisted the man with the cropped head, but he came away from the car and joined the driver. 'But already I am sure what he is doing. This man, what else would he do?'

'We cannot be sure,' the driver said.

The other shrugged and climbed in. Dawlish kept out of sight until the other car had passed, then crossed the sales room again. He felt a quickening excitement which had begun earlier in the day when he had first noticed the little German car. To be dogged by another car, even a smaller one, on a long journey like this was not unusual, but for at least an hour he had felt sure that he had been followed. That was why he had sent Felicity on alone. Now he knew for certain, but Felicity need not be told, at least for the time being. He might even manage to deal with this pair tonight. If he put the car in a garage and then found some excuse to go down to it, he might be with it when these men arrived.

It would be much better if Felicity had no idea that they had been followed.

He whistled softly to himself as he went to the pumps and spoke to a well-dressed man who looked very hot, and who complained bitterly that he could not do everything, and the two boys were away. 'No, this was not an agency of the Jaguar car, only of French, German and American cars. The Jaguar agency was in Rue Capucines, which was . . .' he explained volubly and pointed right and left, and Dawlish found the directions easy to follow.

The English car agency was in a narrow street, and looked much smaller than the first garage, but the white-smocked man in charge spoke excellent English.

Had he seen this Jaguar car?

But yes, he said, it had been driven through two days ago, heading south. He himself had seen it, and on previous occasions had filled the tank and serviced the car, when the owner was staying in Fontainebleau. He was an antique dealer, was he not?

He looked astonished at Dawlish's surprise, shrugged, and watched Dawlish walk away.

The grey Volkswagon passed, with the driver and passenger looking very straight ahead, as if they were not the slightest interested in Dawlish. He stepped into a narrow street and saw a café on a corner, little more than a *bistro* with a few tables outside, and a girl ready to serve coffee and slices of a big cake with a shiny brown top. He stepped inside. The inevitable mirror advertising a vermouth was at the side of the café, and he could see the garage and the Volkswagon, which had stopped. The passenger jumped out, and went to the garage. A flabby-faced man slopped up to Dawlish in carpet slippers.

'*Café, si'l vous plait.*'

'*Oui, m'sieu.*'

'*Toute de suite.*'

'*Ah, oui, m'sieu.*' The man shuffled off, and Dawlish was able to study the mirror for perhaps five minutes. Then the passenger came back, moving very quickly, and giving the impression of great excitement. He jumped into the little car, which roared off. Dawlish put a fifty-cent piece down on a table marked with wet wine bottles of a hundred seasons, and hurried back to the man in the white smock. He grinned when he saw the other's expression.

'What is this all about, *m'sieu?* First you ask me about the car, then these men ask me what it is you wish to know. You are a policeman, perhaps?'

'No.'

'They are not policemen,' the man said with fine scorn.

'Did you tell them what I wanted?'

'But yes, *m'sieu.* Was there anything wrong in that?'

'Nothing wrong at all,' Dawlish assured him. 'A thousand thanks.' He waved and smiled and hurried back to his car. There was no possible doubt that the two men were checking on him because they thought that he was tracing the movement of Macklin's Jaguar.

What was the best way to deal with them?

For the first time he almost regretted that he was in France; in England he could take many more chances, because he was so well known. Here he had to be law-abiding, or . . . He had once seen the inside of a French jail because of an excess of zeal, and did not want to repeat the experience. But there must be some way of making sure that the two men from the Volkswagon talked.

He would have to bring Felicity into this now; they would hatch up some scheme together. He had been a fool to think there was any reasonable possibility of keeping the discoveries from her; she would know the moment she set eyes on him that he had news.

He went quickly back to the car. It was only half an hour since he had left Felicity, and there was no point in sitting parked in blazing sun for another half-hour. It would be worth finding out if he were followed again. He drove round the town, which was thronged with people crowding into the shops, and gave the impression that he was trying to find his road. Two *gendarmes* at a fork in main roads waved him on furiously. He watched in his mirror, saw no indication that he was being followed, and went slowly back to the palace. Most of the coaches had gone, and there were far fewer people. Parked on the other side of the road were several grey Volkswagons, but from here he could not see the registration plates; the important thing was that he could not see the driver or his passenger.

Ten minutes before she was due he saw Felicity; her hat was unmistakable even a long way off. Dawlish got out of the car and went to a position where he could see her best, just for the pleasure of seeing her walk; that always did him good. She was nearing the gates, and any moment now she would surely look up and see him—if she could see anything or anybody under the brim of that hat.

She did not see him.

He would have crossed the road to join her, but a stream of traffic came, and he waited impatiently; he was never really at home with the traffic on the right, and liked to take more care than in England. The stream seemed never-ending, but it was all on his side of the road. Felicity came into the road, and then saw him—and her face lit up. It was a moment when they forgot Gillian Kelvedon, her mother, Ivy Marhsall and the whole problem; they had no thought for anyone but each other.

The traffic thinned; Felicity was waiting for an old motor-cycle to pass. Dawlish stood by the Lagonda, hand on the door to open it for her.

He heard the snort of a car engine, but that was not unusual here. He wasn't looking anywhere but at Felicity. She glanced towards the left, the right way for her to look, and stepped towards him. As she did so, the snort of the car became a roar, and made her jump and stop in the middle of a pace, and swing round in the other direction.

Dawlish saw a grey Volkswagon bearing down on her.

He could not see the driver, but in that moment of awful fear, saw that two people were in the front of the car.

'Get back!' he bellowed at Felicity. '*Back!*' But she was caught in two minds and off balance, and he knew that she would never be able to get out of the way.

He leapt forward.

As he jumped, he saw the Volkswagon come frighteningly close. His arms were spread wide to envelop Felicity. She was swaying backwards. He flung his arms round her and hurled himself forward, carrying her with him. There was no opportunity to control how he fell, little hope that he would avoid the small car altogether, and he waited for the impact, for the snap or crunch of bone. He felt a sudden tug at his foot, that was all. He lay at full length, Felicity still in his arms, the roaring of the engine in his ears. He heard other sounds, as of people shouting, and the shrill blast of a *gendarme's* whistle. He felt Felicity move. He wanted to get up and race after the Volkswagon and wanted desperately to make sure that Felicity was not hurt, but it was difficult to move, and he believed that the car which had nearly run them down must be miles away by now. Then he felt hands touching him. He let Felicity go, and began to get to his feet. Felicity's hat was lying a few feet away from her. Her face was very pale, and there was a shocked look in her eyes. She had bumped her head, of course, and been almost stunned. He was helped to his feet, and two men and a girl began to help Felicity. A *gendarme* came hurrying, white baton swinging, words pouring from him.

'Did you see who it was? Has the car stopped? Is the lady hurt? Is——'

'It was a Volkswagon, grey, with a Paris registration,' Dawlish said, as quickly as he could. 'Can you stop it, please? Can you——'

'Oh, it will be stopped! These madmen of drivers, they cause an accident, they drive on, they are imbeciles and there is no other word for them. Are you hurt, sir? Your leg. . . .'

Dawlish felt something peculiar about his right heel, and could not understand it; it was not so much pain as strangeness. He forgot that as he went to Felicity, who was being brushed down by a little American woman in a black and white check dress, who was saying:

'Wasn't that a wicked thing to do, Andrew? It's just criminal to drive an automobile like that. Are you sure you are not hurt, ma'am? The way that big man saved your life, why, that was the most wonderful thing I ever saw. Wasn't it the most wonderful thing, Andrew?'

Felicity was looking at Dawlish. Dawlish was conscious of her gaze, knew that she was asking the obvious question: *had* it been an accident? If he told her the truth, then they would have fear by their side for the rest of the journey; yet what had happened made it even more imperative to go on.

He twisted round and looked down at the back of his right shoe—and saw the cause of the trouble. The heel had been wrenched off. But except for a bruise and a graze or two, that was the only injury or harm done. It would be easy to laugh, but there was no promise of laughter in Felicity's eyes, for she was thinking the same as he: if this had been an attempt to kill, would the killers soon try again?

9

"Accident"

'I'M all right,' Felicity said. 'Can we go somewhere quiet, Pat?'

'Yes,' Dawlish said, and took her arm. 'Let's get over to the car.' He guided her across the road while one of the *gendarmes* held up the traffic in each direction, and two others followed Dawlish with great eagerness and readiness to help. A little old Frenchman sprang forward and opened the door for Felicity. A boy in absurdly short khaki shorts came bounding along, holding his right hand high and calling, '*Voici, voici!*' As Dawlish stood back for Felicity to get in, the youth handed him the heel of his shoe, and bowed with great solemnity.

Dawlish thanked him gravely.

In good French he explained to the *gendarmes* that his wife was suffering from shock and that she must rest. He would be at the Hotel de la Poste, his name was Dawlish—he spelt that out—and that he hoped the police would find the lunatic who was in charge of a car. '*Imbecile*' was exactly the right word; the policemen repeated it with suitable gesticulations, the small boy repeated it with a hiss, the courteous old man muttered it. Dawlish got into the car and started off, with fifty people waving him goodbye and two hundred more watching him; a stream of traffic, a hundred yards long, began to crawl after him.

'Sure you're all right, Fel?'

'I'm a bit shaken, that's all,' Felicity said. 'Are you going to stay here?'

'For an hour or two, anyhow; you need a cup of tea.

The Hotel de la Poste is the only one I've noticed, I think I can get there without losing the way.' He turned a corner and glanced back, and saw the long-legged, short-panted lad racing after him, waving Felicity's yellow hat aloft. He slowed down and then saw the hotel, not far along the narrow street. He drew up outside it as the lad turned the corner and came running like a hare.

Felicity saw him as she got out, and smiled.

'Now I know you're not feeling good,' Dawlish said. 'You ought to be in a panic because you nearly lost your hat.'

'Pat——'

'I'll get a room for a couple of hours, in spite of what they'll probably think of us,' Dawlish said. He took her in firmly, with the lad still racing in their wake. *Madame* was at her counter, outlined against a small window. There had been an accident, Dawlish explained, and his wife . . . and before he could finish the boy burst in, waving the gay hat, and talking vigorously and excitedly, explaining in a few sentences all Dawlish wanted to say.

He offered the lad a hundred-franc piece, and the boy beamed and refused it. The black-clad proprietress took them upstairs to a large room, more bower than bedroom, with huge roses on the wallpaper and soft green paint on the woodwork and a huge double bed of brass. The boy hovered. He would watch the car, and if there was any way in which he could help he would be delighted; it had been most exciting.

'Ah!' said Dawlish, and Felicity saw from his expression how quickly his mind was working. 'There is a thing you can do,' he said to the boy, 'but it must be secretly done, you understand?'

Fine bold brown eyes glistened.

'I understand perfectly, *m'sieu!*'

'The driver of the car which nearly killed my wife—he is a small man, and with him is a man who looks like . . .' Dawlish described them both graphically. 'Did you see the car itself?'

'Yes, *m'sieu!*'

'It is just possible that it is still in Fontainebleau,' Dawlish said. 'If it is, I would like to talk to that driver myself, and without the police to hear what I have to say to him.' He winked. 'You understand?'

'Completely! And it will be a great pleasure. I would like to say a word to that driver myself, the imbecile. I am very glad madame is not badly hurt.' The boy smiled at Felicity in a way which showed real admiration, and went out, closing the door very quietly behind him.

Felicity was sitting on the edge of the bed.

'I've often had a worse fall than that and not felt so silly after it,' she said. 'My head's pounding.'

'Shock,' Dawlish said.

'Is it what I think it is?'

'No accident,' Dawlish announced.

'Then——'

'They've been following us most of the day,' Dawlish said, 'and they went to inquire at the garage where a man saw Macklin's Jaguar two days ago. There isn't much doubt that they want to stop us. With you badly injured, I would be stopped.'

Felicity said, 'I see.' She lay back on the big, square pillow, and looked up at him from under her lashes. 'When did you first realize this?'

'This afternoon.'

'Can you get the police to help?'

'I doubt if any policeman would agree that it was deliberate,' said Dawlish. 'But it was hit and run, and they'll have a go all right. If we try to make it attempted murder they'll think we're just being British. And they'll almost certainly want us to stay for a bit, so that the magistrates can talk to us. I think I'll telephone the Yard and tell them what happened; they might be able to have a word with Paris, and Paris might pass a word on. But we don't want to waste time, do we?'

'I suppose not,' Felicity said. 'Pat, what do you think it is all about?'

'It would be easier to say what it isn't about,' Dawlish said. 'It isn't simply a case of a *roué* bringing a pretty girl to the Continent, and it isn't just a case of elopement. We are not meant to find Macklin.'

Felicity made no comment, and did not even look as if she wanted to say that she wished they had not come. She was still very pale. Dawlish heard a rattle of cups, opened the door, and admitted *madame* herself, smiling in a pleasant way and carrying not only tea and cups and saucers, but a hot water jug, milk, and biscuits. She placed all this on a table by the window, said '*votre service*' as if the whole thing really was a pleasure, and went out. Dawlish handed Felicity her handbag, and she took out two aspirins as he poured out tea.

'Did you suspect anything like this when we left England?'

'I hadn't a notion; just the fear that it could be another Ivy Marshall,' Dawlish answered. 'The police still don't know who killed her and why she was killed.'

Felicity sipped tea.

'Pat,' she said, looking up, 'I think you ought to try to make Bill Trivett convince the Paris police that this might be the same investigation. They're bound to put their backs into it then. Will you?'

'Yes.'

'In my hearing,' Felicity insisted, and Dawlish grinned and promised that she should be with him at the telephone.

. . . . .

'All right, Pat,' Trivett said, his voice loud and clear. 'I'll talk to the Sûreté at once, but it's really only guesswork, and they'll realize it. They might say they won't move until we've some evidence. Anyhow, I'll emphasize this hit and run, with a British citizen involved. Where can I find you tonight?'

'The garage chap said that the Jag was on the Sens road, which means Sens, Auxerre and beyond. I'm going to plump for Auxerre for the next inquiry,' Dawlish said. 'It's on the best road to the coast, and there's a small English car agency there.'

'Sounds reasonable,' Trivett admitted. 'Look after yourself, Pat, and look after Felicity.'

'That's what Felicity prays,' said Dawlish. 'Thanks, Bill.' He rang off, and turned to look at Felicity who was sitting on a high stool in the small office where *madame* had left them on their own. Felicity had a better colour. It was two hours since they had arrived here, and Dawlish was anxious to be on their way.

'I expect the boy to be back by now,' he said, 'but we can't wait all day for him. I'll leave a message. *Madame!*' he called, and the woman in black came hurrying.

Ten minutes later, Dawlish and Felicity were in the car. Dawlish looked in the driving mirror, but saw no sign of the boy. He could picture him now, first holding the heel aloft, then holding the hat. Nice eager lad, he would be disappointed at finding Dawlish gone, but the thousand-franc note left at the hotel would soothe his feelings a little. Dawlish started off, and a Renault turned into the street and came hurtling towards them, as if it meant to pass and reach the next intersection first at all costs. Dawlish pulled to the right. The Renault's tyres were screeching, and Felicity had a scared look as she twisted round to see.

Then Dawlish saw that there were police in the car. He stopped. All four doors opened at once, and three uniformed and one plain-clothes man stepped out; the plain-clothes man short, sallow, and with flashing eyes. He was sorry, but he wanted to see M. Dawlish at the commissariat; he would not detain M. Dawlish for long. He was enchanted to meet Madame Dawlish, and humbly apologized for inconveniencing her. Dawlish towered above all the men, who surrounded him as if he were a modern Gulliver and gave him the firm impression that they meant to make sure that he did not escape.

'You wait in the bar, sweet. I won't be long,' he called.

'Can't you make him invite me, too?'

'Madame, I regret,' the plain-clothes man said, flashing his eyes and teeth. 'It will only be the little minute.' He waited for Dawlish to squeeze himself into the car, where he sat scissored up, while two other men crowded in beside him and two others went to the front. The car started off as if it were after a lap record at Le Mans, swung wildly round several corners, ignoring other traffic and yet miraculously avoiding all threat of accident. Then it pulled up outside the police station. Dawlish, expecting to be taken before the magistrate to make a statement about the car, followed two of the uniformed men and the plain-clothes men along murky passages, until he was ushered into a room which was not only full of shadows but very cold.

This was a morgue.

Dawlish's pulse began to beat faster. The plain-clothes man raised his right hand to switches on the wall, and went *click, click, click!* Each click brought a flood of light at one section, and each light shone straight down on to a stone slab—and the fourth on to a shape, covered with a sheet, which draped a stone slab.

'If you please,' the plain-clothes man said, and took him to the head of the slab. There was the shape of a human body, tall and slim—too tall, Dawlish thought, for either the driver or the passenger of the Volkswagon. 'You will tell me, please, do you know this person?' the plain-clothes man said, and with a dexterous twist of his wrist, pulled back the sheets.

The long-legged, eager-eyed boy lay there.

. . . . .

'It is now certain that Dawlish will have told the police everything,' Andrew Sharp said to the man who had driven the Volkswagon. They were in a café on the outskirts of Fontainebleau, about the time that Dawlish saw the dead body. 'So we must make sure that Macklin and this Gillian girl go quickly. Macklin could do us a lot of harm—and he has friends *en route*. Get after them quickly.'

'And Dawlish?'

'Dawlish also, if he looks like getting too close to Macklin,' said Sharp. 'Your mistake was to attack the Dawlishes and the boy, but—it isn't important; the important thing now is to make sure that Macklin and the girl are put out of the way. Don't let Macklin suspect—let him make his usual contacts until you can catch up with him.'

10
Facilities

'How did it happen?' asked Dawlish, and thought that at least the pale face was unscarred; and hated as he had seldom hated in his life.

'An accident, *m'sieu.*'

'A motor accident?'

'Yes.'

'A Volkswagon?'

'It is not known what car,' said the policeman. 'It is known only that it was a narrow street, there was no room for two cars to pass, and this poor boy was found in the middle of the street—crushed to death. It surprises you?'

'It surprises and shocks me.'

'Why?'

'Because . . .' began Dawlish, and explained what the plain-clothes man obviously knew already: that the boy had seen the earlier accident, had come to see him and Felicity. He could not make up his mind what to do or say beyond that. If he told them that he had sent the boy to look for the Volkswagon, then the police would almost certainly want him and Felicity to stay for the night, might even detain them for several days: French legal processes could be very slow. Dawlish wanted police help without causing a hold-up; help and facilities so that he could keep after Macklin, not be kept away from him.

Yet he had sent that boy to his death.

He knew that his expression betrayed the cold hatred he felt for the killers. That was not all. There was the acuteness of danger for Felicity and for him; and there was the virtual certainty that Gillian Kelvedon was in the hands of murderers. He could not play this like a game; these were brutal facts. He knew, too, that the plain-clothes man suspected something of his dilemma, for the man was looking at him in the cold light of the morgue, while the body of the boy lay between them.

'You have some statement to make, *m'sieu*?' the plain-clothes man suggested, more gently than he had spoken before.

'Yes,' said Dawlish.

'So. Thank you, M. Dawlish.' The teeth flashed. 'It is not often that we have the pleasure of meeting an eminent criminologist; we are very honoured to have you in Fontainebleau.' The bold eyes positively glowed with amusement as the man twisted back the sheet and covered the pale face of the boy whose life had been cut off. 'This way, please.'

Dawlish wondered how much he knew.

He sat in a small office, smoking a French cigarette, studying the little detective while telling his story—everything from the first time he had heard of Gillian Kelvedon; there was nothing which Dawlish kept back. Occasionally the detective made a note; more often he nodded, grimaced, pulled at his lips, shrugged, and made little snorting comments.

'So,' he said at last. 'I am glad you have told me all of this, M. Dawlish. Some of it, of course, I know. Your friends at Scotland Yard talked to my friends at the *Sûreté Nationale*, and it comes to us on the teletype machine, so we are not surprised to hear about you. As your description is so easy to identify, M. Dawlish, I want you to understand that you are among friends,' the smile flashed. 'There are some things which one cannot do officially, but to those who served us during the war, to those who worked with the Resistance—can we not turn the blind eye? Tell me what you would like to do.'

Dawlish said, 'So you know nearly all there is to know about me,' and smiled as if ruefully, but his heart was beating faster with the near certainty that he would not be compelled to stay here. 'I want to trace that Jaguar and find out when it was last seen on the road.'

'I shall send the request out,' the detective promised, 'but it is not easy, especially in these days with less formalities at the border. Good for the holiday peoples, and good for the criminals also. And there are many Jaguars in France; it is easy for us to trace one, but Germany, Switzerland, Austria, Italy—so many places by now. I will send out the request, however. And you—you will be very careful, M. Dawlish.'

'Very.'

'This Miss Kelvedon'—he pronounced the name carefully—'do you know her well?'

'No.'

'Are you here just to search for her, or is there some other good reason?'

'I don't know what this is all about,' Dawlish said, 'and I started out looking for a girl who was in trouble. Now I've other reasons, M. Corot. Is there anything more I can tell you?'

The detective stood up smartly.

'I do not think so.' He rounded his desk and thrust out his hand. 'It is the great pleasure to meet you. If it is possible to find how this boy died and who killed him, I will inform you. I shall arrange for your car to be reported as you pass through towns and villages; we do not want to lose you, my friend. I say again, be very careful.'

Dawlish shook hands.

'In Auxerre there are some very good hotels, and the food—it is the best in France!' The detective kissed the tips of his fingers. 'I commend to you the Hotel de la Poste, also the Hotel de L'Épée and de la Fontaine. But they are all good! *Au'voir m'sieu.*'

Two uniformed policemen went back with Dawlish, the driver much less reckless this time. Felicity was sitting at a table outside the hotel with a tall glass in front of her; she jumped up as the car stopped. Dawlish saw her pick up his shoe, and saw that the heel had been put on again. She held it rather as a cudgel, and it looked incongruous against a pale green dress and a big hat which was exactly right for her.

Now he had to tell her about the boy.

The police saluted and drove off, with Madame peering from her cubby hole. Dawlish took Felicity to the car, turned in his seat and watched her face as he told her. He did not want to make the slightest mistake with Felicity. It was a long time since she had been involved in such a mission, and already she had been badly shaken. What did she really feel, now? Ten years ago he would have taken it for granted that she would want to go on with the chase, that she would not dream of suggesting that he ought to leave this to the police, but now—he knew that of recent months, especially, she had been quickly alarmed, more anxious to keep him at home, more sensitive and nervous.

He finished the recital.

Her expression had changed very little and told him practically nothing, although she had watched him as steadily as he had watched her. After the first shock of the boy's death she seemed to have schooled herself to accept the rest of the story. Watching so intently, Dawlish realized how deeply he loved her; how completely they had grown together over the years. He felt a surge of mingled dread and rage at the fact that she had nearly suffered the fate of the boy now on that cold slab.

'What do you want me to say, Pat?' she asked quietly.

'Exactly what you think,' he said.

'I wish we had never set out on this,' Felicity told him very quietly, 'and if I'd known what was going to happen I don't think anything would have persuaded me, but—he was such a nice boy.'

Dawlish said, 'And I killed him.'

'You'll always feel that you did until you find out the real reason for it,' Felicity agreed. 'We'll have to go on.'

'Fel, I wondered if . . .'

At last she smiled.

'You wondered if I would like to go back home and wait for you, because you'll be able to move much more freely without me! *No*, Pat. You're stuck with me.' She hesitated for a moment, then went on very deliberately: 'We might still be able to save Gillian Kelvedon, mightn't we?'

So she also accepted the probability that Gillian was an intended victim.

Dawlish began to ask the obvious question more loudly, too: why should anyone want to kill Gillian?

'At least we can feel that we can always go to the police,' Felicity said.

'They won't all be as co-operative as Corot, but we shall probably strike a good one next time we need it,' Dawlish agreed, and realized the inanity of the remark as soon as he had made it: the truth was that he did not know what to say for the best. He started the engine as Madame came to the door, and waved to them. He reached the next corner, where three schoolboys, one long-legged and wearing absurdly short shorts, were strolling along, carrying their satchels. He noticed how Felicity looked at them. He turned into the road to Sens, and saw a girlish-looking woman with a baby in her arms scolding another boy, not so tall but very long-legged. He stood first on one foot and then on the other.

Dawlish glanced at Felicity and saw the tears in her eyes.

He was glad when they were past the outskirts of the town and he could put his foot down heavily on the accelerator. What little traffic there was going in their direction went quite slow, and he hurtled past car after car, the wind hissing and rattling about the windows. They stared straight ahead, with the forest on either side at first, and then with the open countryside, the flat farming land which was visible for mile upon mile in all directions. There were the farm horses, drawing cutting machines as if this were a century ago. Here and there they passed huge fields of corn already nearly ripe, in other places great fields of golden stubble. The sun shone hotly upon them.

The needle touched the hundred and stayed there for at least two minutes, until Felicity said:

'Not quite so fast, darling.'

'Sorry.'

'I hope it's not going to be a waste of time,' Felicity said. 'How long will it take us to get to Auxerre?'

'At this rate, three-quarters of an hour,' Dawlish answered.

The fifty-odd miles took them fifty-one minutes. He slowed down on the outskirts of the town, saw the bypass, and left it on the left. Soon they passed the turning to the market place, and a sign reading: Hotel de la Poste. 'That's one the chap at Fontainebleau recommended,' Dawlish said, 'and there's plenty of parking room up there.' He swung off the main road up the steep incline to the market, and reversed so that the back of the car was almost opposite the hotel door, but the hotel was on a different level, and there was a small road outside it. 'Coming with me—or shall I see if they've room before you get out?'

'I'll come,' Felicity said.

They went down to the hotel, Dawlish taking out the photograph of the actor, and a dapper man came forward from the dark interior of the little entrance porch.

'Yes, *m'sieu*, there is a nice room . . .

'Yes, *m'sieu*, of course I know M. Macklin. He has often stayed here—he is the dealer in the antiques. Only two days ago he stayed here with his wife. I tell you something—he was married in Auxerre, in this very town. And mam'selle—she was so very lovely.'

Felicity was staring at him so intently that he seemed almost embarrassed. Dawlish uncovered the photograph of Gillian, and the hotelier said at once:

'Yes, that is mam-selle—or now I should say, that is madame! Yes, certainly.'

'Can you take us to the *M. le Maire* to inquire about this marriage?' asked Dawlish.

'But of course, that is no trouble,' the hotelier said. 'Wait please, and I will send a boy with you.' He delved into the darkness of the restaurant, vanished through a doorway, calling "Pierre, Pierre!" Soon he came back, dapper and slightly out of breath, with a thick-set boy wearing long jeans and a singlet, and looking slightly as if he were covered with flour. 'You will take *M'sieu* to the house of the mayor,' he said. 'Hurry, please.' The man looked at Dawlish. 'And you will require the room for the night?'

It was nearly seven o'clock.

Felicity was looking tired out.

'Yes,' said Dawlish. 'Darling, why don't you go up to the room, and——'

'Don't be silly,' Felicity retorted.

Twenty minutes later Dawlish studied the entry in the registry book. There was Gillian's name and signature, quite unmistakable, and the short, bearded mayor, who looked far too young for his office, enthused about her. He also explained that M. Macklin had a special licence to marry—he lived in France for the requisite time; he, *M. le Maire*, had often seen him in Auxerre. M. Macklin was engaged in the buying of antiques, and often he called at the three shops in Auxerre where one might expect to find such things. There was, also, some trouble with his motor car, a garage man had mentioned this, but *M. le Maire* was not sure how serious. The garage was on the outskirts of the town. Dawlish made a note of the addresses of three antique shops, and sent the boy back to the hotel.

'That's one good thing—he obviously made an honest woman out of her,' Dawlish said. 'If we hadn't run into that trouble at Fontainebleau I would say that it's a wild goose chase.'

Felicity made no comment, and Dawlish drove to the garage. It was on the right, and there were the usual Shell petrol signs, one or two enamel notices offering service to several makes of English car, and a huge tin shed where half-a-dozen cars were in various stages of repair. Outside was the wreck of a grey Volkswagon, rusty with age, and a huge pile of old, smooth, tyres. Two men were working inside the garage, one looking too young to handle tools efficiently. He came towards them, quiet looking.

'*M'sieu?*'

'We are looking for a friend who drove through here

two days ago in a Jaguar car,' Dawlish explained, carefully. 'We are told that he came to you for some repair.'

'That is so.'

'Did our friend tell you where he was going next?'

'No, *m'sieu.*'

'Do you know what road he took?'

'No, *m'sieu.*'

'What car was he driving?'

'An old Renault, *m'sieu.*'

'Was there any serious trouble with his own car?'

'Yes, there was.'

Dawlish asked sharply, 'How serious?'

The youth shrugged, backed inside, and pointed. Dawlish followed him, and saw the shiny Jaguar standing in a corner, its bonnet up, and half the engine open to view. He went over to it, Felicity tagging on behind him.

'What was the trouble?'

'A faulty distributor head,' the youth explained promptly.

'Couldn't he get a replacement, or repair?'

'It was necessary to send to Paris,' said the youth.

'Has the spare been fitted now?'

'Yes.' The youth's dark eyes had no brightness in them and he seemed to resent the questions more and more. Dawlish went closer to the Jaguar. There was nothing at all the matter with the engine as far as he could see, and he studied the distributor head for several minutes, looking at it first from one side and then the other. The youth stood by, glowering. Dawlish turned suddenly, gave him a broad smile, and took Felicity outside. In the hot evening sunshine he said:

'That's not a new distributor head; that's the old one.'

'I don't understand,' Felicity complained.

'There was nothing wrong with the car,' said Dawlish. 'Macklin left this one here in case it was being looked for, and went off in an old Renault which will be a hundred times more difficult to pick up. Don't say it,' he added grimly. 'Once the number plate and the *Departement* number was changed it couldn't be traced. Macklin knew there was danger when he got here, and knew he had to switch cars.'

'Then——' Felicity broke off.

'It's going to be a worse job than ever tracing them,' Dawlish said, 'but at least we can send a cable to Mrs. Kelvedon; the marriage seems genuine.'

'Would Macklin marry her if he were planning to kill her?' asked Felicity, slowly.

'We can't even start guessing at his motives,' Dawlish said, 'but we've got to try to find out where he was going to next. I think this is a case where I must telephone Corot and ask him to persuade the police to open this garage man's mouth.'

He saw that the youth was watching them sullenly as he drove off. Ten minutes later he was at the hotel, talking to Corot.

'We shall find the full description of that Renault and we shall make sure it is sent to every Departement,' Corot promised briskly. 'Congratulations, M. Dawlish. I regret I have no good news for you, however. The Volkswagon and the two men in it have not been traced. I repeat—you will be very careful, won't you?'

'Find that Renault, and there won't be any need for caution,' Dawlish said, and a moment later he rang off. 'Sweet, can you wait for dinner until we've called at the antique shops?' he asked hopefully.

'Let's go,' said Felicity.

11

Second Change

'HAPPY?' Macklin asked.

'Wonderfully, wonderfully happy,' Gillian said.

'How do you like France?'

'I've always liked what little I've seen of it,' Gillian answered, 'and somehow you never know what you're going to come across next.' They were climbing a steep hill towards the town with a great church dominating it, almost forbidding in the evening light. On the other side of the road was a network of irrigation canals, and people working in the fields which were intersected by the canals. They were travelling slowly, and the engine of the Renault was knocking badly; Macklin had to change gear suddenly and force the stick home.

He grunted.

'I don't think this will see us through,' he said. 'I'll have to hire another car.'

'Oh, what a nuisance!' Gillian exclaimed in consternation. 'If only the Jaguar hadn't broken down.'

'Can't be helped,' Macklin said, 'and with luck we'll get a better one than this. Won't be quite so easy, though. If we'd had the Jag to leave as security, so to speak, we could have rented anything up to a Cadillac, but with this we shall probably have to manage on a motor scooter. Mind?'

'Provided I'm with you, I'll hitch hike!'

'I believe you would,' said Macklin. 'But it won't be as bad as that. I think the best thing is to get to a hotel and settle in, and then you can have a bath while I try to fix a car. Right?'

'If you think that's best.'

'I must say you're the most dutiful wife—' Macklin began, and then broke off suddenly, and changed gear again, jammed on the brakes, and jolted Gillian forward. 'Sorry. I thought the damned thing was going to collapse on me.' He went up the hill more slowly than ever, passing labouring cyclists, passed by several cars which swept by. 'There's one good thing, we can spend two or three hours here in the morning. I've a couple of people to see, and one of them might help with a car if we get into trouble.'

Gillian said, 'What's Bourges like, darling?'

'Depends which way you look at it,' said Macklin. 'It's got some big munition factories—parts of it are almost like the Saar and the Ruhr—but there are Frenchmen who will tell you that it's the real heart of French art.' He grinned. 'If you see what I mean. The usual mixture in this part of France. Roman ruins and medieval buildings stuck on top, bad plumbing and perfect food. You can look through the cathedral and the museum while I'm making my calls in the morning. Okay?'

'I might be a great help to you in business.'

Macklin laughed: 'No, my darling, you don't do any work on this honeymoon. Remember, you won't ever have another!'

Gillian laughed. . . .

She had never been more light-hearted, and this time she did not even mind when he left her in the hotel room overlooking a small cobbled square, crowded with people gathered round stalls which were still open for trade—mostly selling sweets. She had a sense of age and of grandeur here. She slipped out of her dress immediately, stripped, put on a flimsy dressing-gown, then turned on the bath before going to the window again. She saw Clive walking across the square, threading his way between stalls, and his fair hair was caught by the evening sun. No one else with fair hair was in sight. He stood out among them not only because of that but also because he was taller than most, and he walked so well. He reached a corner, turned it, and then came back and looked towards the hotel.

She was startled.

He wasn't smiling, but frowning. She had never seen him look like that before; it was almost as if he had some great worry which he hid from her, but which he could not hide when he was on his own. Then he caught sight of her, and his expression changed and she saw his teeth flash as he waved. A moment later he had gone.

'It must have been imagination,' Gillian told herself, and turned away from the window, saved the bath from overflowing, and got in. The water was almost cold, but the day was so warm and she felt so sticky that it did not matter. She kept picturing Clive's expression as he had turned that corner. Should she tell him what she had seen? Or would it be better to pretend that she had noticed nothing?

She wanted to be at the window again to see what he looked like when he came back, although there was no way of guessing how long he would be, and she did not want to hurry; now that she was used to it, the water was pleasant enough, and it was good not to feel too hot. One of the troubles was the old car, of course; it would be much better if he could get a newer one.

It was a strange coincidence to have two cars which did not go properly.

Probably he hadn't spent enough money on the hire of this one.

She found herself frowning, and told herself that if Clive caught her looking like that he would probably think that she had some secret hidden from him. Her face cleared, and she actually laughed, and lay at full length in the bath, looking down at the whiteness of her body, feeling the water playing about the hair at the back of her neck; she need never worry about getting her hair wet, when it dried it would look as neat and feathery as ever. She felt almost as if she could doze; and then she giggled. It wasn't really surprising that she should be tired! Tomorrow morning they could lay in, though. She didn't want to go looking round stuffy old cathedrals.

Or should she?

It was nearly half-past seven before she was dressed, and Clive still wasn't back. She kept glancing out of the window, but didn't see him. Most of the stalls had closed and been wheeled away, but three were piled high with sweets which looked absolutely luscious. There was a cool breeze at the window now, too.

'I'll go and meet him,' she decided.

She went downstairs, hatless, moving slowly so that she could be sure not to get herself too hot again. She had almost forgotten that change in Clive's expression until she neared the corner where he had disappeared.

He was coming out of a shop which was crowded with old furniture. There were some large chandeliers in the window, and a huge mirror which reflected everything which passed outside. He had no idea that she was watching him. His eyes were narrowed and his lips were set tightly—viciously was the word which came to her mind. He hardly looked like the same man.

Then he looked up and saw her.

. . . . .

'I hope she didn't see me,' Macklin muttered.

He was finding it a great strain—much greater than it had been when he had travelled rather like this before. There was the memory of Ivy Marshall leering at him all the time, contrasting so evilly with Gillian's laughter and radiance.

He had never known anyone so happy as Gillian.

Now, he turned the corner after waving to her, and hesitated outside the shop which was filled with furniture. Over the window was the name *Monet & Cie, Objets d'art*. The shop front wanted painting, and he knew that the interior was in worse condition. At the far end of the shop, sitting at a small desk, was the older partner, Monet himself, a silvery-haired man who wore a monocle. He looked up as Macklin went in, a smile of welcome dawning. When he saw who it was he jumped up and came with both hands outstretched.

'M. Macklin, what a pleasure it is to see you again!' He gripped hands, and looked as if he would gladly have kissed Macklin on either cheek. 'I thought perhaps you would not be coming?'

'Why not?' Macklin demanded.

'The last four visits have been from others,' said Monet. 'But perhaps you have had a holiday, eh? What is it I can do for you this time?'

'I'll look round,' Macklin said, and tried not to sound gruff. 'Is there a message for me?'

'Yes, it is in the safe. I will get it at once.'

'Thanks,' Macklin said. 'And there's something else you can do for me.'

'Name it, please.'

'I need a fast car which I can use for about a week.'

'Oh, there is no problem about that,' responded Monet. 'I shall arrange it for you with the Garage Centrale—you know where that is?'

'I would rather you arrange it, without saying who wants the car.'

'It shall be done,' Monet assured his visitor, and turned round. 'You will excuse me, please, and I will obtain the message which is waiting for you.'

He went through a small door at the back of the shop. Macklin stood looking about him, at the heavy furniture, with here and there a valuable or interesting piece, one or two rococo pieces which made him wince. There was a small nineteenth-century coffee table, with curved legs, and when that was polished and cleaned it would look delightful. His expert eye appraised it, but after a while he turned and stared moodily out of the window. Then Monet came back, carrying a letter which looked exactly like the one which he had received in Auxerre.

'If you will stay here for ten minutes I will arrange the car,' Monet promised him.

Macklin nodded, waited until the man had gone out, and then opened the letter. It was headed Paris, like the other, and it was considerably longer.

You are being followed and it is essential that you shake off your pursuers. It is a tall, fair-haired man, named Dawlish, who is with his wife, who is also tall and between colours. Dawlish is a very powerful man of about forty-five years, his wife about four or five years younger. Dawlish speaks French well, his wife a little. They are travelling in a Lagonda capable of great speed.

They are acting on behalf of Mrs. K. and so far as we know their interest is only in G.K. They must not be allowed to talk to her. You know what that means. Your mission must be completed as quickly as possible, and you should then return to Paris for consultations.

Again the signature was a scrawl which no one could recognize.

Macklin wiped the sweat off his forehead with the back of his hand, then with a handkerchief. He moistened his lips, which were very dry. He sat on the small desk, the letter open in his hand, and slowly he crumpled it up. People passed to and fro, but their footsteps hardly sounded through the window and the door. He went into the big room at the back of the shop, which was crowded almost from floor to ceiling with old furniture, much of it dusty, most of it very large. Against one wall was a small Arab door, beautifully studded. He ignored all this, but went to an old cylindrical iron stove, which was cold. He opened it, set a lighted match to the letter, waited until it was half-burned, and dropped it on to the dry ashes in the stove. Then he replaced the rounded plate at the top, rubbed his hands together, and went outside. The name Dawlish meant nothing to him, but that word "mission" was like a death-knell—his, as well as Gillian's. There was no doubt that Sharp meant exactly what he said.

But—must he obey?

He loved Gillian, didn't he?

But the man Dawlish made the situation ten times worse.

Then Monet came back, and said briskly:

'I have arranged it, my friend. A new Simca, which can take you at a hundred and fifty kilometres an hour if you desire it.'

'That's good,' Macklin said. 'That's fine. Thanks.'

'Are you quite well, *m'sieu*?'

'It's hot in here,' Macklin said, and Monet shrugged as if he knew that was not the true answer but would not press him. He went out. Two minutes walk away there was Gillian, but he could not bring himself to go and see her. He went towards the heart of the town and the cathedral. He passed several more antique and *objets d'art* shops, and three shops with artists' work displayed in the windows. In spite of the cooling breeze he felt very warm. He walked to the top of the hill leading to the cathedral, hesitated, and then went inside. It was very cool. The evening sun caught one of the stained glass windows and transformed it, and the many colours tinted the air and the light everywhere. An organ was being played, softly. Three women were bowed in front of an altar where a dozen candles burned steadily, spreading their yellow red glow. He went towards these and hesitated by the stall where a nun was waiting patiently for customers who would buy candles, post-cards, rosaries and the little knick-knacks which would be prized as souvenirs. Macklin was sweating. He bought nothing, turned away, paused by the offertory box, and put in a folded thousand franc note. The nun watched him with calm eyes from the other side of the nave.

He went out again and walked down the hill, retracing his steps until he was near the corner and Monet's shop. He wished he had gone the other way, but it would be a long way to turn back. As he neared the doorway he saw Monet waving furiously, obviously to attract his attention, so he stopped. Monet came out, small face alive with satisfaction.

'I catch you,' he said, 'and that is very good. I have another message for you, by telephone.'

'Yes?' Macklin asked, and now dread was cold in him.
'It is that the situation has become more urgent, your friends are in Auxerre. Do you understand it, *m'sieu*?'
Macklin said stiffly: 'Yes, perfectly, thanks.' He turned on his heel—and then saw Gillian coming towards him from the corner, fresh in a white dress with a black design on it, hatless, her eyes glowing until she saw his expression.

12

Need for Haste

'CLIVE!' Gillian exclaimed. 'What's the matter? What's worrying you?'

He didn't respond.

'Clive!'

'It's all right,' he said, and tried to make himself smile, gave up, and screwed up his face. 'I've a dreadful headache, darling. I thought the fresh air might help, but it's getting worse.'

'Oh, darling, you should have stayed in the hotel.'

'I—I didn't want to worry you,' Macklin said, and he saw the way her face cleared, and knew that for the moment he had satisfied her. He took her arm. 'Let's go back. I'll have a wash, and sit back for twenty minutes, then we'll have dinner. I may be hungry; we didn't have much lunch, did we?'

'That was my fault,' Gillian said. 'I wanted to have a real appetite for dinner. Would you rather go straight in and eat now?'

'I'll try some aspirins first,' Macklin said. 'Darling, you have a stroll round. It's lovely out, and you'll give the citizens of Bourges quite a treat.'

She laughed in spite of herself.

'I have managed to do one thing,' he told her. 'I've made arrangements about the car.'

'Wonderful!'

She went with him to the hotel steps, and he wondered what he would do if she insisted on coming upstairs; he could easily lose control of himself. But she saw that he wanted to be on his own, and so she smiled and turned away, saying:

'Half an hour, then.'

'Not a minute longer,' he called.

He watched her walking across the uneven cobbles. A car swung round a corner into the square and she hesitated, as if its wild speed scared her. The driver swung well to the right. Gillian quickened her pace until she reached the far side, and it was as if she did not intend to allow herself to be scared again. She went to one of the stalls where stuffed sweets and marzipan, nougat and fresh chocolates were being sold from great piles, and the attendant spoke to her. She shook her head; she probably hadn't any French money, Macklin realized.

He went upstairs.

The words of the letter seemed to be hovering about his mind and the words of the telephone message almost screamed at him. His "friends"—this Dawlish—were in Auxerre, only half a day's drive away. Who the devil was this man Dawlish? If things had gone normally, there would be at least a fortnight for the situation to work itself out. Was there such a man as Dawlish, or had Sharp made him up, so as to bring pressure to bear? The man was quite capable of doing that.

Could he save Gillian now?

Or must he overcome his feelings for her?

This Dawlish was in Auxerre, remember; and Sharp could prove that he, Macklin, had killed Ivy Marshall.

But Dawlish was in Auxerre.

Would he find out about the marriage? Would he find out anything from the garage? Had he any idea where to go next?

If the Dawlish's arrived in Bourges it would be disastrous, because it would mean that they knew what route he had taken. But what chance had they of finding him here? He had changed cars. Even the police would find it difficult to trace him, for beyond Auxerre he had changed the plates, so that the car had taken on a Cher registration; no one would suspect a car registered in the *Departement*. There was no immediate need for fear, and the arrival of the

Dawlishs' car at Auxerre must be due to luck. He tried to convince himself of that, but could not. He looked out of the window on to the square. Gillian had gone. An English car came sedately round a corner, and his heart began to pound, for it looked like a Lagonda. The fool in Paris hadn't told him what colour Dawlish's car was; this was a green one. It—no, it wasn't a Lagonda, it was a Bristol, he always confused these models.

Sweat stood out on his forehead.

He went into the bathroom, stripped, got into a cold bath, shivered, and then lay still. Gillian had been here only a few minutes ago. Warm, soft, lovely Gillian.

He had killed Ivy Marshall, and he had to face the possibility that he must kill Gillian, whatever his own feelings, because his own life would be at stake if he did not. Sharp would be ruthless; he could be sure of that.

But the fact that this Dawlish was after him, too, seemed to worsen the danger for him. If Gillian were found dead there would be a hue and cry immediately, and there would be nothing that he would be able to do to save himself. He must face facts. Sharp would make sure that he could not betray him; he would kill first. Whichever way he, Macklin, looked there was disaster, unless he could take Gillian to some place where her body would not be found. God! What an awful thing to have to do!

Could he?

If—if he didn't love her, it would be easy, just the law of survival.

With anyone else, for instance, there were Souillac's caves. He knew them well, had visited them several times, and knew that behind the main grottoes there were deep fissures in which a body could lie for months, perhaps for years. But people were continually in and out of the caves. There were occasional roof falls which entailed repair work and the shoring up of the roof though; it would not be safe.

The mountains between here and the sea ?

It would be easier to get lost in these, but he needed to lose himself completely. He simply dare not be seen with

Gillian anywhere near the place where her body would be found.

He hardly realized that he had already conditioned his mind to what he must do.

The important thing was to get a long way from Bourges quickly, he reminded himself. They must leave tonight, not in the morning. Gillian would be disappointed, but on the empty road at night he could put hundreds of miles between him and Dawlish, and there was no reason to believe that Dawlish would travel by night. He must break the news to Gillian after dinner; they could be on the road by ten o'clock, pass through Chateauroux and Limoges, and be at Souillac by the morning, pull in by the side, kill——

'But if Dawlish suspects me, when Gillian doesn't turn up, they'll name me to the police,' Macklin said.

Oh, God!

'Shall I let the Dawlishes catch up with me, and then deal with them?' he asked himself. 'Dare I?'

. . . . .

Dawlish paused outside the little antique shop round the corner from the market at Auxerre. It was dark inside, and filled with junky-looking furniture—more like a second-hand shop than an antique dealer's. Felicity was looking into a small dress shop next door. It was the quiet hour, for the shops were nearly all closed, and most people were in at their evening meal.

'Is it locked, darling?' Felicity asked.

'Looks like it,' Dawlish said, and tried the door handle. To his surprise the door opened, and there was the shrill clangour of a bell. He stepped inside. Felicity stayed near the dress shop window; he could always trust her not to obtrude too much. He heard footsteps at the back of the shop, and the door opened to admit a heavily-built, sullen-looking man; had there been any light at this end of the shop his face might not have looked so gloomy and hostile; now he looked almost bestial.

Dawlish smiled brightly, and explained.

He was looking for a close friend of his who was interested in antiques and *objets d'art*, and was very anxious to find him. He might have called here in the last day or two —a M. Macklin. The man shook his head almost before Dawlish asked the question. 'Here is a photograph of him,' Dawlish added, and took the picture of Tod Benson, the film star, out of his pocket. 'Will you come to the light, please?'

'I have not seen him.'

Dawlish smiled again, and dipped his hand into his pocket; a thousand franc note rustled. The man stayed back in the shadows and said:

'He is English?'

'Yes.'

'No Englishman comes this week or last week. I have not seen him.' He ignored the proffered note, and turned and went back into the recesses of the shop. Dawlish hesitated, shrugged his shoulders, and turned to go. He reached the door, as Felicity looked in and waved to him. He opened the door and stepped out, pulled the door to and gave it a sharp shake; the bell rang wildly as it would if he had really closed it; but he had left it ajar. Felicity, seeing what he was doing, did not come nearer.

'Come in if anyone else is coming,' he said.

'What are you going to do?'

'Have a look round.'

'Pat, be——'

He grinned. 'Careful!' He turned back into the shop and tip-toed towards the back door; for a large man he could move very softly and silently. Not ten miles from here, during the war, he had made one of his many parachute drops into Occupied France. He reached the door and peered in the crack between the door and the frame. A room was filled with junky furniture, and another open door showed. He stepped through, and heard a strange, faint hissing noise. He could not understand it, so he stood absolutely still.

The noise persisted.

He stepped closer to the partly open door, and saw the surly man standing, sideways to him, and polishing a table; a bottle of French polish stood on a shelf near him, and he was rubbing the surface of an eighteenth-century card table as if it were a labour of love. There was a strong smell of polish, slightly astringent.

Dawlish pushed the door wider open.

The man jumped, and swung round.

'Hallo!' said Dawlish brightly. 'I didn't expect to see you again.' He smiled and stepped forward, and the man thrust the table to one side and leapt at him. The sullen face lit up with an expression of spiteful anger, and his clenched fists looked as if they were strong enough to kill a man. Dawlish simply moved to one side, and the other's wild swing sent him off balance. Dawlish put out a leg and tripped him up. He banged his head on the metal at the corner of the table, and grunted. When he stopped moving he was leaning against the wall, one hand on the floor, mouth agape, looking almost imbecilic.

'Where did he go?' Dawlish asked, and took out the photograph again.

'I—I have seen no one!'

'He was here yesterday,' Dawlish asserted. It was a guess, but he thought it would probably convince the other man, and he saw the uncertainty which glittered in the pale, unintelligent eyes, or the eyes which masked intelligence, 'Where did he go?'

'I—I do not know!'

'He was here?'

'Yes.'

'What did he want?'

Those eyes masked the man's intelligence all right; the direction of the questions convinced him that Dawlish did not know as much as he tried to make out. The man began to get up, and Dawlish let him. He saw the way his victim edged towards the shelf where the bottles were, and had no doubt what he would try to do. He let him get within a hand's reach of the nearest bottle, and then struck at him, two powerful blows to the stomach which brought his head jolting forward, then one to the chin: the kind of boxing which he had learned in his youth and the kind of blow with which his own nose had been broken. The man sprawled back over the table, his hand went flat on it, and smeared the fresh polish.

'Where did he go?' demanded Dawlish.

'It is no use asking me,' the man gasped. 'I do not know!'

'What did he want?'

'Always—a message.'

'Where from?'

'*I do not know.*'

Dawlish said, 'Was there a message for him yesterday?'

'Yes.'

'Did you see it?'

The pale eyes shifted for a moment, and then looked back at him squarely.

'No.'

'You opened it, and read it, and sealed it up again,' Dawlish said. He smiled. 'Would the sender of the message like to know that?'

'*No!*'

'So you're frightened of him,' Dawlish reasoned. 'You ought to be much more frightened of me. What did the message say?'

The man muttered, 'It just had a name on it, the name of a town, Bourges. That is all I can tell you. It is everything.'

'Where would he go in Bourges?' asked Dawlish, and now he stood over the man with his fists clenched, and he must have looked as if he were capable of murder. The helpless man in front of him could not know that he was picturing a lanky lad on a cold slab; and picturing the beauty of Gillian Kelvedon.

'He might go to M. Monet, of Monet & Cie,' the man told him, gasping. 'He might——'

Then Felicity called from the second doorway: 'Pat, two men are coming. They just got out of a Volkswagon!'

13

Three Birds

THE big, sullen, frightened man was breathing heavily; it was almost a snore. Felicity appeared in the doorway, fresh and vivid against the gloom of the background, and obviously scared. A motor scooter roared outside.

'Out of a Volkswagon,' Dawlish echoed. 'Well, well. Did they see you?'

'I don't think so.'

'Good job you weren't wearing that hat,' Dawlish said, but there was no gaiety in his voice or in his eyes, for he was seeing the boy's body beneath the cold light of the morgue; and he was remembering that if these were the men he had seen at Fontainebleau, then they had almost killed Felicity.

'*Do* something!' Felicity cried; and now footsteps sounded outside, 'Pat, what——' she broke off, and he saw that she was nearly in panic. That was because she had been so shocked earlier in the day; she wasn't really herself.

'Yes,' Dawlish said. 'Go and see what's at the back.' He spoke quite calmly, while gripping the Frenchman's arm and twisting it behind him so that the man could not move. Felicity hurried, tripped against the leg of a Louis Quinze chair which poked out, fell against the back door, and then went out.

The shop door opened with a clang of the bell.

The Frenchman opened his mouth to shout.

'Hush,' reproved Dawlish.

There were only seconds to play with, and he dared not throw even one away. All or nothing was in the punch which he drove upwards at the other's chin; and the satisfying *ugh* and the dull thwack of his knuckles on the fleshy chin told him that he had not forgotten how to knock out a man with one blow. He heard men speak in undertones as he hooked his victim's legs from under him, lowered him, and pushed him underneath the big table which he had been polishing. No one coming in from the front shop could see him. Dawlish heard the footsteps of the two men, and stepped swiftly behind the door. He heard Felicity moving; she appeared at the back door for a moment, and he put his fingers to his lips. She mouthed something which he did not understand, and he waved her away. She dodged out of sight as one of the men called out:

'Pierre, are you there?'

'Come in, sir, come in,' Dawlish called, in French which was good enough to pass muster. Unsuspectingly, the men pushed the door wide open and stepped in; and the first had a round head and dark, close-cropped hair. He came right in, startled at what seemed to be an empty room, and the small driver followed, a pale and pinch-nosed man. He hovered on the threshold, and Dawlish tripped the first man up and pushed him, to make room, caught the other's wrist and pulled him inside, and then kicked the door to.

'All right out there, Fel?' he called.

'There's a kind of yard and a lane leading to one of the main streets,' Felicity answered. 'Are you——'

'Come in, lock the back door, and then go to the shop so that you can tell me if we have any more visitors,' Dawlish said. He spoke and acted quite calmly, as if these were the most natural circumstances anyone could imagine. He had hardly glanced at the two men from the Volkswagon, one of whom was leaning against the table, his foot close to Pierre's head, and the other standing in a corner, head thrust forward, as if he wanted to throw himself at Dawlish but could not find the courage. He was the driver. He was breathing hard, but the man with the cropped hair seemed not to be breathless; he was watching Dawlish from very bright, narrowed eyes.

'You will regret this,' he declared.

'I haven't the slightest doubt of that,' said Dawlish, 'unless I change my mind.'

'You change your mind?' Puzzlement sounded in the man's voice.

'At the moment I intend to leave you alive,' Dawlish said. He saw the driver start, saw this man's eyes narrow so much that they were almost closed. 'That's more than you did for the boy in Fontainebleau, and more than you wanted to do for my wife.'

'I do not know what you mean.'

'Don't you?' asked Dawlish softly. 'You'll find out.' He glanced at the door as Felicity came in, and he felt quite sure that the man would try and trip Felicity up and so take him off his guard. 'Stay there, Fel. I was just about to ask our friends which one of them killed Ivy Marshall.'

The name came out so very casually, but there was nothing casual about its effect. The narrowed eyes widened for a moment, as if the man with the cropped hair was astounded, while in the face of the smaller man there was less astonishment than fear. For a moment all of them stood looking at one another, and Dawlish's face was set and grim.

Felicity said, with a sigh, 'So they *are* the same men.'

'They're the same men all right,' declared Dawlish. He put his right hand to his hip pocket and drew out a small automatic. He held this on the palm of his great hand, and it looked absurdly small. He moved it so that he held the handle, and pointed it, as if nonchalantly, at the driver, for he thought that man's nerve would break first.

Even Felicity, looking at him, was appalled by the bleakness on his face; he had the look of an executioner.

The driver exclaimed: '*No!*'

'Turn round,' Dawlish ordered, and the man obeyed almost too quickly, kicked against Pierre's foot, and tripped. There was Pierre to take into account. He would not be unconscious for long, but he could not get up from beneath the table without warning them, and he did not constitute any immediate threat.

'Hold this, Fel,' Dawlish said, and handed her the gun. 'Be careful with it, I haven't a licence and it's illegal to bring firearms into France.' He ran his hands over the thin body of the driver, drew out a flick knife, dropped it into his own pocket, and stepped to the man with the cropped hair. He felt quite sure that this man would not give in without a fight. He saw him tense his body ready to throw himself forward; he let him begin, and then drove his right fist into the man's stomach. The blow was so savage that it jarred his arm and shoulder.

Felicity winced.

The man groaned and dropped in his tracks.

Dawlish glanced at Felicity with a grin, then went down on one knee and ran through the other man's pockets. He found another flick knife, that was all. He took this away, then looked through the contents of the man's pockets—a wallet containing a thick wad of paper notes, all kinds of oddments, but nothing which was likely to help him in his search, nothing with a name on it. He ran through the rest of the pockets, but there were no papers. The man was now beginning to move, grunting and groaning. Dawlish stood up slowly, and then spun round on the driver—and the man backed away in fear.

'Where is Gillian Kelvedon?' asked Dawlish, very clearly. 'Don't lie, and don't waste time. Where is she, and where is Macklin?'

'I only know they have gone to Bourges. Macklin will be at the shop of Monet & Cie. That is all I can tell you; I swear it is everything.'

'Is she alive?'

'I can only tell you that they were to go to Bourges. I swear that is all I can tell you.'

'Did you kill Ivy Marshall?'

'No, I did not,' the man almost shrieked. 'I did not kill anyone, I——'

'You killed that boy in Fontainebleau.'

'It was not I, I did not intend to kill him, just to frighten him. It was Georges.' The scared eyes darted towards the man on the floor who seemed to be holding his hand hard against his stomach, as if to ease the pain. 'I was driving, he swung the wheel, I could not stop him.'

'Why did he do it?'

'The boy had been asking too many questions, he saw the car, we saw him examining it, so——'

'Where will Macklin go after Bourges?'

'He will go to Monet in Bourges; there he will get a message! He obtained a message to go to Bourges, that I can tell you.'

'There's a lot more that you can tell me,' Dawlish said harshly. 'Why was Ivy Marshall murdered? Why did Macklin take Gillian away. What is this all about?'

The man was sweating.

'I do not know, I am only the driver. I do what I am told, that is all. Sometimes I drive the car, sometimes I drive the truck, sometimes I collect from such shops as this one, but I do not know more than that. Georges——'

'Pat,' Felicity interrupted.

'Half a mo', sweet, I——'

'Pat, we mustn't stay here any longer,' Felicity said firmly. 'I don't think you'll find it easy to make the other man talk, and we have to drive to Bourges. Can't you hand these men over to the police?'

Dawlish looked at her very thoughtfully, and then began to smile.

'Yes,' he answered. 'Yes, we can shut 'em up in here and let the police know that the Fontainebleau police want them for a hit and run job. Thanks, sweetheart. I'll try to keep on the ball in future. I wonder where is the best place to hide.'

'There's an old shed at the back crammed with furniture,' Felicity told him. 'It's got a padlock big enough for a bank.'

'You really are earning your keep,' enthused Dawlish. 'Is it locked?'

'Yes, but I shouldn't think you'd find it hard to open.'

'Nothing being impossible,' said Dawlish, and bent down and tugged at Pierre's arm. The heavy man was no longer unconscious, but he preferred to pretend that he was.

Dawlish twisted him round so that he could get at the trousers pockets, felt the chink of metal, and drew out a bunch of keys; three of them looked like padlock keys. 'Try these,' Dawlish said to Felicity, and as she took them he looked round the crowded room and saw some strips of canvas webbing, used for upholstering chairs. He stretched out for this, and it was conveniently cut into short lengths. He bound Pierre's mouth with it, then tied his hands, and did the same with the other two men. The face of the man with the cropped head was a greenish yellow, and obviously he was still in pain.

The boy in Fontainebleau wasn't.

Felicity came in. 'It's open,' she announced.

'Coming,' said Dawlish. 'Watch this pair.' He dragged Pierre to his feet and pushed him towards the yard. Pierre went forward sluggishly but without a protest. The shed was made of thick planks of wood and the door was steel reinforced; Dawlish noticed that as he pushed Pierre inside. The furniture was so badly stacked that there were little paths along which one had to squeeze in order to get to the far end of the shed. Pierre was too solid to squeeze easily, and Dawlish heaved a chest of drawers to one side, and made room. Then he went back for the other two men. The driver was able to walk to the shed, but Dawlish had to carry Georges.

When they were all inside, Dawlish studied the steel reinforcement of the door and the heavy iron poles which strengthened the walls from the inside. He knew that Felicity would soon be stamping her feet with impatience, and he also knew that she was right: they had to drive to Bourges through the night; there was just time for a hurried meal.

'Pat, don't waste time.'

'No time wasted,' Dawlish assured her. 'What is there peculiar about this situation?'

'You standing there day-dreaming!'

Dawlish grinned.

'Oh, no, my sweet,' he said. 'Whatever else, I don't

day-dream with you.' He gripped her hand, slammed the door, locked it, and weighed the bunch of keys in his hand. 'Tell you what. Go back to the hotel, tell them how sorry you are—the right word is desolated—ask them to have us a good steak and *pommes frites* ready in twenty minutes. We'll have a bottle of that Côte du Rhone 51, too. Make them realize that we're really in a hurry. Then take the car and get it filled up—by the time you're back at the hotel, I'll be there: we can be off in an hour.'

'All right,' said Felicity, as if she knew that it would be useless to argue.

She hurried off, and Dawlish went through the room at the back of the shop and stood there for a moment in a way which Felicity would have found infuriating. He examined several pieces of furniture for secret compartments, for he was already wondering if Macklin really acted as a carrier of some illicit goods. Next he picked up two chairs which had broken legs. He put one of these on the newly polished table, and examined the breaks; they seemed genuine enough: he looked round and found another chair which needed polishing and which had three sound legs and one which had recently been repaired with a new piece screwed in. When the polish was finished, all four legs would look genuinely old.

'It can't be a fake antiques racket; they wouldn't kill for that, would they?' he asked of the dingy shop. He raised the mended chair and smashed it down on the once broken leg; and the joint split, the leg came right off. He picked both chair and leg up, and saw that the join had never been solid; both leg and chair seat were hollow.

Inside them were small metal cylinders, about the size of small cigars.

Dawlish said, 'Well, well,' and put two of these in his pocket, then hurried out.

14

Secret

THE Volkswagon was parked just round the corner, and Dawlish paused for a moment, the two metal cylinders nestling in his pocket, then bent down and took the valve cap off one tyre, pressing his thumbnail against the valve itself, and heard the hiss of air. It was at least a minute before the tyre was flat, but no one appeared to notice him from the nearby windows, and no one came down the street. He walked on and saw a priest in dark robe and wide-brimmed hat walking briskly along on the other side of the street.

'Excuse me, father.'

The priest stopped. 'Yes, my friend?'

'Can you tell me where I will find the police station, please?'

'Oh, it is near,' the priest said, directed him, and then asked with a dry smile, 'Is there any help that I can give you?'

'Plenty I need, but none that I have time for now,' Dawlish said.

'Find time, one day,' urged the priest.

The police station was in an old building and a *gendarme* stood outside. There were notices stuck on boards near the front door; the whole atmosphere was like that of an English police station with a hint of the prison about it. A perky little man greeted him, was affable, and led him to a large room where a man in plain clothes sat at a large desk behind which was a huge map of the district. This man was tall and grey-haired, and smiling a little sombrely as he stood up.

'I am happy to meet you, Mr. Dawlish.'

'Oh, no,' breathed Dawlish.

'You are surprised that I should recognize you? My

friend Corot of Fontainebleau was on the telephone to me twice already, and he told me that it was possible that you would come to see me. There is only likely to be one man answering your description in Auxerre at the same time. Please, sit down.' He motioned to a chair. 'You will smoke? A cigar? A cigarette . . .'

'I have to be back at the hotel in five minutes,' Dawlish said. 'My wife and I are driving to Bourges tonight, because I think that might be where Gillian Kelvedon is.' He spoke with great precision, and his expression as well as his tone drove away the smile of welcome from the other man's face. He took out one of the cylinders, and placed it on the desk. 'I found that in the leg of a chair at the shop of Pierre Flambon, in——'

'Rue de Cloche—I know it well.'

'I'm told that Macklin might call on a shop called Monet et Cie, of Bourges,' Dawlish went on, 'and I want to get there as soon as I can. But if you go to Flambon's shop, and look in the shed at the back, you will find a lot of furniture and some men. Two of the men were in the hit-and-run Volkswagon which Corot would like to find, and it's round the corner at the Rue de Cloche, with a flat tyre.' Dawlish stood up quickly. 'Ask them why they killed Ivy Marshall, will you?'

The plain-clothes man said heavily, 'So it is definitely the same case.'

'Yes,' Dawlish assured him. 'If it weren't for the marriage I would expect Macklin to kill the Kelvedon girl at a given moment, perhaps at a given signal. It's as well to assume that the marriage won't necessarily save her. It's possible that he might kill her more quickly if he believes that the police are on the look out for him. It won't help him to leave this girl alive if he can be charged with the murder of Ivy Marshall, so he is more likely to kill. That's why I want to go on with my wife and find Macklin. I might be able to find out what's driving him on. I might even find out if he is really in love with this girl. Will you ask the police at Bourges to give me all the help they can?'

The plain-clothes man was untwisting one of the metal cylinders and looking at Dawlish at the same time. Dawlish's question came out at exactly the moment that the cylinder came apart. He pulled the two ends away, and a smaller cylinder, like a cigarette, fell out. The policeman broke the paper and there was a tiny trickle of white powder. As deliberately, he wetted the forefinger of his right hand, touched the powder, and put it to his tongue.

'Yes,' he said quietly. 'I will arrange for you to have all the assistance you require, Mr. Dawlish. You know, of course, that this is cocaine.'

'I think it would be worth while examining all the furniture at Flambon's place, and all the furniture at Monet's and other shops where Macklin is known to call,' said Dawlish. 'The driver of the Volkswagon will be more helpful than the other man, whose name is Georges. Don't let them escape, will you?'

'They will not escape,' the detective assured him.

As Dawlish passed the end of the Rue de Cloche less than ten minutes afterwards, a grey van pulled up outside the antique shop and the doors opened at the back and men who looked more like soldiers than police jumped out. People stopped to stare. Dawlish strode on to the hotel in time to see Felicity get out of the Lagonda, parked in the market place again and headed towards the road. She waved and waited for him.

'All set?' he asked.

'They have promised to have the steak ready the moment we get in,' Felicity said. 'I've packed everything.'

'I don't know what I'd do without you,' Dawlish said. 'Hungry?'

'Famished.'

'That's a nice healthy sign, anyhow,' remarked Dawlish. 'So am I. I feel better, too—at least I don't feel that boy's death won't go unavenged. We know what it's about now.' He explained to her in undertones as they entered the hotel and as they waited for the steak; that came in less than three minutes—huge, beautifully fried, with a dab of butter on it, and a dish of golden brown *pommes frites*, another of *haricots verts;* and there was cut bread and a dish of butter which made it look appetisingly cool. A waiter came up and poured the wine. 'What we really need is half an hour to sit back in,' Dawlish said. 'But——'

'Won't the police be able to make sure that nothing happens to Gillian now?' asked Felicity.

'I wouldn't like to rely on it,' Dawlish said. 'If Macklin knows that he's on the run he'll be away from Bourges by now, and he might have switched cars again. That's going to be our main trouble. And he might drive through the night, too.'

'How can he know that he's on the run?' asked Felicity.

'These people aren't fools,' Dawlish said, and then laughed at himself. 'How pompous can I get? Sweet, if they deal extensively in dope, it's big money. It's a country-wide organization, too. Whether this stuff is going out of France or coming in doesn't concern us; the police will look after that. We've just one concern: finding Gillian before Macklin treats her as he did Ivy Marshall.'

Felicity said, 'I think I've had enough to eat, Pat. Can we start?'

She had never known him drive faster; and she had never before wanted him to go faster still.

. . . . .

'Is your headache any better at all?' asked Gillian a little uneasily. They were in the dining-room of the hotel in Bourges, fruit plates and finger bowls in front of them, an empty bottle of rosé wine in its slender-necked bottle between them. Gillian's eyes looked huge. It was pleasantly cool in here, because there was plenty of cross ventilation, and she looked fresh and at her best. Clive didn't. He was sweating at his forehead and his upper lip, and kept breaking off small pieces of bread and rolling them between his finger and thumb into little pellets.

'It isn't, much,' he told her.

'I hate to see you suffering like this,' Gillian said. 'Isn't there anything we can do? If we go to bed right away, and——'

'I can never lie down when I've a head like this,' said Macklin. 'The blood goes to my head and it's agony. As a matter of fact . . .' he hesitated, and then waved his hands '. . . Oh, it doesn't matter.'

'As a matter of fact, what? darling?'

'Oh, it wouldn't be fair,' Macklin said. 'But what does often help is driving—movement seems to do something, and sitting upright eases the pain. There's nothing so restful as a long night drive, but you——'

'Can you arrange to leave the hotel?'

'Oh, yes.'

'Then let's go,' Gillian decided, and her eyes looked brighter already; all she wanted to do was to help get rid of the drawn expression in Clive's eyes.

'You might have to sleep in the car,' he warned her.

'Oh, that doesn't matter! You arrange it at the desk, darling; I'll go and pack. I hadn't unpacked much, anyhow, it won't take ten minutes. I——But what about the Simca car? Will that be ready?'

'Oh, yes,' said Macklin. 'We'll have to drive to the place where it's parked in the Renault and then transfer the bags, but that won't take long. Gillian, are you really sure you don't mind?'

He was quite sure that she would say "no"; as sure from the beginning what she would do when he hinted at driving by night. He could read her like a book, he told himself, she was so naïve it was almost too good to be true—and too bad to be true, also.

He kept looking at her slender neck.

He watched as she hurried out, twisting round to smile at him before she disappeared, and the moment of her smile was one of the worst that Macklin had known. He picked up the bill and took it to the desk, where a wizened-looking old woman in black smiled mechanically at him. She was displeased when he told her he would be leaving, and demanded a payment for the room, which she might not be able to let again. Macklin did not haggle. He went outside where the Renault was parked, and the porter came up, shabby in his white coat.

'Your baggage is ready, sir?'

'Come upstairs in five minutes,' Macklin said.

It was cooler out here, and there was a steady breeze blowing across the square which was empty but for a few parked cars. He strolled to the corner. The wind struck cold against his forehead. He saw Monet's shop in darkness, moistened his lips, and remembered that last message. Monet had not known its significance, of course, had not realized that he had conveyed orders to kill. None of the people who were in the chain of shops across France—and in England and others parts of the Continent, also—knew just how far the principals would go. Only Sharp's chief helpers knew about the murder of Ivy Marshall, for instance. . . .

Poor Ivy.

She would have been alive today had she not found out what Sharp was doing, and confided in him, Macklin. Her bad luck! The mistake had been to kill her in France, of course. He had not wanted to kill in the first place ; he had pleaded with Sharp to allow her to have a chance of life, but Sharp had been obdurate; and a word from him would mean ten years or more in prison.

It was far worse with Gillian, and he did not think that she had the slightest idea that her life was in such danger.

Sharp didn't make mistakes; there must be a compelling reason for his determination that she should not return to England alive. The more he thought about that, the more he faced up to the fact that he had no choice: he could not save her. If he didn't kill her, Sharp would make one of his other men do it, so she was doomed whatever he did. At least he could make her last hours on earth happy. She need never know what was to happen.

When should he kill her?

The vital thing was to make sure that she could not be found by this Dawlish, or by the police. He must have plenty of time to escape. Sharp would help in that. He would have to get across the Med, of course, and live in Algiers or one of the smaller cities. It would be easy enough and pleasant enough, but he wouldn't find it pleasant unless he could get there before the police found him. So—he had to kill Gillian and give himself at least forty-eight hours to get clear: in fact he could use longer, but it might not be possible.

Was tonight the right time?

It would be easy enough, on the road. He could pull up, pretend that he wanted to sleep, wait until she was asleep, and then . . .

Her body mustn't be found for some time. Why didn't he remember that? So it couldn't be tonight, unless there was an exceptional opportunity. He tried to recall what he knew of the road between Bourges and Digne. In fact it was long and straight most of the way; there was little cover.

The grottoes at Souillac would have been better, in spite of the risks. Could he make a detour, and get into them by night, or were they barred? One could never be sure, with the religious grottoes.

He saw a light go on in Monet's shop as he was about to turn round. Gillian would probably be ready by now, and there wasn't a moment to waste.

Monet came out of his shop, hurrying straight across the road, and there was such tension in his manner that Macklin felt sure that he was looking for him, and that he brought bad news. Standing there in the quiet square with the little Frenchman's footsteps ringing out on the cobbles, Macklin could have screamed.

Then Gillian called out from the hotel entrance:

'All packed, darling!'

15

Night Rides

MACKLIN half turned towards Gillian, still hearing Monet's footsteps. The little old man could not hurry as fast as he would like, and the sound of his gusty breathing came clearly.

'Just a minute!' Macklin called.

Gillian would come towards him, of course; why shouldn't she? And if Monet had a message, she would hear it. Did she know enough French to be sure of the words? Macklin doubted it, but could not be sure. Monet drew nearer. Gillian began to walk towards the corner, her heels tapping sharply on the pavement. The porter reached the car and Macklin heard him call to Gillian.

'The baggage, madame?'

Gillian turned round.

Macklin wiped the sweat off his forehead and faced Monet, who was near the kerb. He hated the man, but gritted his teeth to keep back his anger. A street light showed Monet's lined face, set with anxiety, little eyes looking very bright.

'I am glad to catch you,' he said. 'There is another message for you, and very urgent.'

'What is it?'

'You must not go to Souillac,' Monet said.

'*What?*' Macklin gasped the word, and felt as if he could strike the man. In his mind he had been so sure that Souillac was the right place: he could almost see the spot where he could leave Gillian.

'It is the message from Paris,' Monet said. 'You are not to proceed to Souillac and Grasse, but to Digne.'

'Digne?'

'Are you not well?' demanded Monet.

'I'm all right. To Digne,' Macklin echoed, and his heart began to beat faster yet with tension, for that was near the coast, and whenever he went across to North Africa it was nearly always from Cannes or one of the smaller harbours along the Côte d'Azur. This was making sense after all. And in the mountains just behind the coast there were a thousand places to hide the body.

'That is what the message said, and there is also this: that Dawlish probably has discovered you are heading for Souillac and that you have been here.'

Macklin said, savagely, 'Oh, has he?'

'That is the message,' Monet asserted. His breathing was a little easier, but he was obviously anxious, and rested a thin hand on Macklin's arm. Gillian was walking towards them again, and she would be wondering what they were talking about so earnestly, while there was always the danger that she knew more French than she pretended. If she asked questions . . .

'M. Macklin, what is the matter. Is this man Dawlish a policeman?'

Monet actually said: '*Is he of the police?*' so clearly that his voice surely travelled, and Gillian surely heard. She was only a few feet away, hesitating now.

'No, he has private interests,' Macklin answered. 'Thank you for making the arrangements about the car.' He bowed and turned away. Gillian was standing further off than he had realized and there was no certainty that she had heard. The light which had made Monet look so old and sickly made her look beautiful. He forced a smile. 'Hallo, sweet. I thought there might be a last minute hitch over the car, but it's all right.'

'That's good,' Gillian said.

She spoke rather deliberately, and was looking at him intently. Oddly? Had she heard that question after all? Why had Monet been such a fool as to ask it aloud? Monet was scared, of course, because if the police caught up with any of the organization there was a real chance they would catch up with him. The little man was walking back to his shop dejectedly. Macklin took Gillian's arm. The porter was standing by the car ready to open the doors, and Gillian said:

'I hadn't any change for tipping him.'

'Soon fix that,' said Macklin.

He got in a moment later. Gillian sat quietly and looked straight ahead of her. The porter, beaming, slammed the door. Macklin missed his gears, a thing he rarely did, and gritted his teeth so that he should not swear at it, at Gillian, at the night, at Monet. The engine started. He moved off, and Gillian was still silent. He sensed that she was looking at him, but when he glanced round she was staring straight ahead, after all. Her hands were in her lap. She did not ask where the car was, just seemed more quiet than usual, and she hadn't asked whether his head was better or not. He would have to pretend that it was worse for a while—until they were out on the open road, headed for Digne. That was a hell of a long way off: it must be eight or nine hundred kilometres, or over five hundred miles. If he was able to keep his foot down most of the night two hundred would be the limit—two-fifty, perhaps; so to get to Digne by the following evening they would have to keep going most of the time. How would he explain it to her? Why didn't she speak?'

He reached the old garage where the new car was waiting, parked and fuelled and ready; only Monet knew that he would be in it. He pulled up behind it. A cyclist passed, tyres whirring. A motor cyclist roared along and his headlights shone on the two cars, but he did not stop. It was a clear starlit night, but there was no moon. The sound of the crickets came very clear from the fields nearby. Silently they transferred the luggage from one car to the next, and when they were sitting in the smaller Simca, Macklin said:

'More comfortable?'

'Yes.' Gillian still seemed subdued.

'Are you all right?' Macklin asked, shortly.

'Yes.'

Macklin didn't speak again, but handled the controls, then started the engine and eased the car onto the road. He drove very carefully for the first two or three miles, and then began to put on speed. The headlights shone straight along the wide road, and the engine responded as well as he could have hoped. This was better. He relaxed a little, but Gillian didn't seem to relax at all. If she had begun to suspect he might be forced to act quicker than he had expected.

Suddenly, she said: 'Clive . . .'

'Yes, darling.'

'What did that man say about the police?'

Macklin opened his mouth, to shout, to tell her that she hadn't heard the word "police," she was dreaming things up; but he stopped himself. If he denied it, she would be more sure than ever that things were not what they seemed, and he could hardly leave her at the side of the road, on these flat fields. Why the hell did she keep asking questions, anyhow?

'You heard that, did you?' he asked, and was surprised that he could speak so lightly. He actually laughed, 'Shall I tell you the dark secret?'

'Yes, please.'

What the hell was the matter with her? She was behaving like Ivy, the little . . .

'This car isn't licensed,' he declared.

'*What?*' Gillian sounded startled.

'That is the extent of my awful crime,' Macklin declared. 'Monet came to tell me that he hadn't been able to get the car licensed in time, and that it should really be running on trade plates—or what passes for trade plates over here.'

Gillian said in a subdued voice, 'Oh.'

'What did you think he said?' asked Macklin, and although he still managed to speak quietly, there was the impulse to shout at her, to make her tell him what was really in her mind.

'I—I suppose I just heard the word police, and—well, it's silly, but——'

She broke off again.

Macklin gripped the wheel very tightly. His foot was hard down and they were travelling at over a hundred and twenty kilometres an hour. No other traffic appeared on the road, and there was only the tall corn on either side, showing in the headlights.

'But what?' he demanded.

'I know it's silly, but until I've told you, I won't be happy,' Gillian said. 'I wondered if you were running away from someone.'

His heart was pounding and his head was aching almost as badly as he had pretended when they had been having dinner.

'Running away? Why on earth should I?'

'I hadn't got as far as that,' Gillian said, and rested a hand on his for a moment. 'Forget about it, darling.'

'But why on earth should you think that I might be running away?' Macklin's voice was harder.

'Well . . .'

'Come on, tell me,' he ordered, and saw the way she stiffened at the tone of his voice. He must calm her down. He must keep calm himself. This man Dawlish knew that he had been to Bourges, might possibly follow him; he had to be a long way from here before he could do anything to Gillian.

Unless he kept her in the car.

How big was the boot? He hadn't seen the luggage put in.

He was sweating.

'All right, I'll tell you,' Gillian said, and he knew she was staring at him, while he put his foot down even harder and the car seemed to fly along, so that the hum of the tyres was a high pitched whine. 'You changed the Jaguar outside Fontainebleau so that no one could see you, and you did the same here—behaving just as you would if you didn't want anyone to know you had changed cars.'

The little devil, Macklin thought; the shrewd, quick-witted little devil. Sharp knew what he was doing!

'It did seem a little queer, didn't it?' Gillian asked.

'Er-yes. Yes, I suppose so,' agreed Macklin. *He must*

keep calm. 'Funny how a thing like that can build up, isn't it? The trouble tonight was because of the registration. Monet didn't want to drive it through the town because the local police would know. He'll get it all fixed up in the morning, and if we're stopped we will just refer the police to Bourges. Simple, isn't it?'

'Yes,' Gillian said. 'I was silly. Sorry, darling.'

'Forget it,' Macklin said, and forced a laugh.

Forget! He wouldn't be able to for as long as she lived. He felt quite sure that now her suspicions were aroused, and she had demonstrated how observant she was, that there would be other things to make her ponder. For instance, the fact that he had insisted on starting out tonight. Insisted? Was that the word? Or hinted?

Would she realize the truth? Had she simply pretended to be satisfied? What did she think he was running away from, anyhow? Did she know that he wasn't booking into hotels as Macklin, but in a false name? He kept her passport, too. He always registered at the hotels, but—she could have checked for herself. She could have asked at the desk at the hotel here, to find out. If she were suspicious, that was the kind of thing she was likely to do.

'Darling,' Gillian said, and for the first time there seemed some of the old warmth back in her voice.

'Yes, sweet?'

'It's silly, but I'm tired. Mind if I sit back and close my eyes?'

'That's exactly what I hoped you'd do,' Macklin declared, and saw her thrust her body forward, wriggle and shift her position until she was comfortable. He glanced at her again, and then saw that her eyes were already closed. If she did seriously suspect that anything was wrong, would she settle down like that?

He shot the car towards the distant mountains.

. . . . .

'What time did we leave?' asked Felicity.

'Just after eight.'

'How far is it?'

'About a hundred and eighty.'

Felicity sat up. '*Miles?*'

'Kilometres.'

'Oh. It's ten o'clock now, so we should be at Bourges by about eleven, shouldn't we?'

'Earlier, I hope.'

'I think I'll close my eyes for a few minutes.'

'Good idea,' said Dawlish. 'Mind if I do?'

'You look where you're going,' Felicity ordered. She settled down immediately, for she had often dozed in this car, and closed her eyes. Dawlish saw that the speedometer needle was quivering on the eighty mark, but this was a cross-country road, narrow in parts, and he could not average much more than fifty. There had been one long hold-up with a convoy of munitions trucks belonging to the American Army stationed not far away, but since then there had been little or no traffic on the road.

'Pat,' Felicity said.

'You're supposed to be sleeping.'

'I'm just resting my eyes. Supposing they've left Bourges.'

'Why?'

'Don't be obtuse. What would you do?'

'I'm going straight to M. Monet, anyhow.'

'Supposing he won't tell you what you want to know?'

'Let's cross that bridge when we come to it,' Dawlish said, and stifled a yawn. 'We can't have lost much time, and with luck we'll be at Bourges long before they've left. They have to sleep somewhere.'

'I suppose you're right,' Felicity conceded, and for the next twenty minutes she did not say a word.

. . . . .

Nearly two hundred miles ahead, Gillian cat-napped, too.

16

Monet

EVEN in the darkness the giant mass of the cathedral of Bourges showed against the sky, blotting out the stars. Dawlish knew the town slightly, slowed down up the hill, took the right streets more by luck than judgment, and came into the square near the hotel, where the stall holders were by day. He drove straight into the parking place, switched off the engine, leaned back, and stifled another yawn. Felicity yawned with him.

'It won't do,' Dawlish said. 'I doubt if you'll sleep in your bed for a week. At least it's a nice thought that we won't be followed, isn't it?'

'I suppose those men couldn't have escaped?'

'Not a chance in a million,' Dawlish assured her, and opened the door. Immediately he heard footsteps which sounded stealthy. The bright lights on tall concrete lamp standards were on, shedding a false brilliance about the square and on the old hotels which were on the left-hand side of the spot where Dawlish was parked.

'What's that?' Felicity asked sharply.

'A copper,' said Dawlish, and saw a small man swinging his baton and approaching them with measured tread. He got out, and called good night. The policeman quickened his pace, and stared with more than usual intentness at him, then looked inside the car, where Felicity was still sitting and waiting.

Then the *gendarme* smiled, brought his right hand up in a salute, and said:

'M. Dawlish?'

'And I said we weren't being followed,' Dawlish said sadly in English, then smiled. 'Yes, I am Dawlish.'

'I have a message for you.'

'Is it urgent?'

'There is no English person of the name of Macklin registered at any hotel in Bourges,' the policeman answered. 'At the request of the police of Auxerre, every hotel has been visited. There are many English couples, yes, but none of that name.'

'Description?' asked Dawlish heavily.

The man shrugged. 'It is very difficult, *m'sieu*, to judge on such a description. There are many who look like this young couple. There is perhaps one thing to assist. One couple left the Hotel de la Poste tonight, after taking their room and having dinner. They were driving a very old Renault. It was registered in the Cher Departement, but it is possible to change the registration plates quite easily.'

'Which way did they go?'

'They left the town on the road to Chateauroux,' the policeman said, 'and we have requested the police at Chateauroux to keep a watch for them.' He saluted again. 'Is there anything else we can do to help, M. Dawlish?'

Dawlish said, 'No, thank you. You have been very good——'

'Pat,' said Felicity, out of the blue.

'All right, sweet.'

'That man you were going to see—can't the police help with him?'

'Later,' said Dawlish, and the policeman looked from him to Felicity, obviously wishing that he could understand English, and beginning to swing his baton a little. 'We shall try to obtain refreshment at the Hotel de la Poste,' he answered.

'Yes, *m'sieu*. They will be willing to assist you, the porter is on duty all night. Oh, *m'sieu!*'

'Yes?'

'There is one other message, from Auxerre. The three men whom you saw earlier tonight.'

Dawlish said more sharply, 'Yes.'

'They are under arrest.'

'Ah,' said Dawlish. 'That's a great relief.' He beamed. 'Thank you.' He opened the door for Felicity, the policeman stood back and saluted again, and Felicity stretched, stiffly, before they went across the square to the hotel. The light shone brightly outside, but it looked cavernously dark within. Yet as they neared it a white-coated porter appeared, a young but tired-looking man with sleek dark hair and a sallow face, obviously expecting them to want a room for the night. Dawlish handed him a thousand-franc note, and he brightened up at once. 'First, we would like to wash, and then we would like to eat,' Dawlish said.

'You require a room, sir?'

'Perhaps,' said Dawlish. He took out the photograph of Tod Benson and the full-face one of Gillian, and held it in front of the man. 'Have you seen these two people?'

The porter took one glance.

'Yes, sir,' he answered. 'Only tonight they were here, only tonight they left here. M. Lane.'

. . . . .

'I've got to see Monet quickly,' Dawlish said. 'I don't want to leave it to the police. They don't know exactly what's on; I shouldn't think Corot or the Auxerre chap was too explicit. If the police here talk to Monet he's bound to close up, and the only real chance we have of getting anything from him is a little private visit. I'll slip out and go and try to get into his shop.'

Felicity said uneasily, 'It's an awful risk, Pat.'

'Not really,' Dawlish said. 'Not so big a risk as with Flambon at Auxerre, unless Monet has other men with him. These people are two short already.' He stood up from the table in the little room set aside for breakfasts, finished a cup of coffee as he stood up, and went on, 'You stay here this time.'

Felicity didn't argue.

Dawlish went out. The porter was sitting in the small office behind a glass partition, and he looked as if he were asleep, but when Dawlish glanced round from the door he was watching him. Dawlish beamed, and passed. Except for the parked cars, several of them with British number plates, the square was empty. The buildings around it were all white-faced from the garish street lamps, but the narrow streets leading off looked like black alleys. He went briskly across the road to the first corner, hoping that Monet's place was near, but not expecting to find it so quickly. He walked past it, took a narrow alley that led off this street, and now walked on tip-toe. He reached another alley, and knew that this must lead to the back of Monet's shop. If Monet were involved in the drug-running, like Flambon, he would have a very guilty conscience. Dawlish stopped by some tall wooden gates at a spot where the alley was just wide enough for a car. There was a padlock on these gates and an iron bar, the kind of protection Flambon used. He walked past, and saw no way of getting into the yard behind Monet's shop except climbing that wooden fence, and it would probably have barbed wire at the top.

Dawlish went back to the alley at its narrowest point. He was able to stretch up to the top of the wall here. He edged along until he was near the big doors, then hauled himself higher and looked into the yard beyond. It was so dark that he could not see much, but he could make out the shape of a shed. He strained his arms as he hauled himself still further up, until he was squatting on top of the gates then took out a torch and shone it cautiously. There were no exceptional precautions as far as he could see. He lowered himself, dropping the last two or three feet. He landed on uneven cobbles and his ankle turned, sending a sharp pain shooting through it, but the pain did not last for long. He shone the torch about, glancing up at the dark windows of this building and the buildings all about it. There was no sound. He saw the padlock on the shed door, and saw that the door and the walls were very solid, as if Monet knew the value and the danger of the commodity he traded in.

There was a back door to the buildings. Dawlish went to it, tried the handle, turned and pushed—and found that the door yielded. That startled him. He pushed more heavily, and the door opened wider, squeaking. He waited, listening intensely, and a motor scooter roared past in the main street; this yard seemed to catch and trap the sound, and for a few moments it reverberated deafeningly. As it faded, Dawlish strained his ears again, but heard nothing more.

He stepped inside, closed the door, and shone his torch about an old kitchen with a big sink, an old pump which looked as if it were still in use, a high open fireplace with hooks hanging from it; this was more like a farmhouse than a house in a city. There was another door within arm's reach, and he pushed this open, too, still wondering why the back door had been left open.

Would one of these shopkeepers be careless?

He thought of the padlocks and told himself that it wasn't conceivable. The double doors had been securely locked; perhaps Monet thought that was sufficient precaution. Dawlish went to the back door again and examined the lock; it was a strong mortice, obviously fitted on recently, and no one would have taken the trouble to do that if they thought that the double doors were a sufficient protection.

Frowning, Dawlish went into the house itself. The pitch darkness of the first passage was relieved a little when he opened a door which led into the shop, for some of the light from the square shone in here and showed the old furniture, one or two glittering pieces, a better place than Flambon's in some ways, but with very much the same kind of stock.

Then Dawlish heard a sound.

He raised his head sharply, and looked round towards a narrow staircase. Someone had moved upstairs. Did Monet live alone? Had he been over-optimistic when talking to Felicity? He listened for a repetition of the sound, began to try to persuade himself that he had imagined it, and then heard it repeated. But he did not think it was a movement; it was more like a moan.

Was someone trying to fool him?

He turned to the stairs and shone his torch up them.

The beam shone on to a shabby carpet and the dark wood at the side of the narrow staircase. Then it faded into the misty darkness of a landing. He started up, and was near the top when he heard the sound again. It seemed to come from his right. There was still a chance that someone was luring him upstairs. He reached the landing and stepped towards the only open door he could see; that sound was not likely to come from a room with a closed door. He stepped close to the open door, and then pushed it back sharply against the wall. It banged noisily, but there was no other sound afterwards until, when he stepped forward, the moaning came again.

This time he switched on a light.

He saw an old man lying on the floor by the side of a huge double bed, a man in a pale-coloured nightshirt which was spattered with blood from a wound in his head. He seemed to be unconscious. Dawlish hesitated, then turned and thrust open the doors which were closed. Two showed furniture storerooms, one of them was another bedroom. He went back to the old man and bent over him, feeling for his pulse, and when he touched it he felt sure that Monet—if this were Monet—would not live long.

Had Macklin done this?

Dawlish stood up. A doctor must be brought here within a very short time, but if he hadn't broken in, Monet probably would not have been found until morning; he could steal a few minutes. He ran through a bureau in the bedroom, an ornate French piece, and found nothing which helped at all. He was startled when a clock chimed, and looked round. He saw a telephone close by the clock with a notepad on it, and he stretched out for the pad. On it, scribbled in pencil, were three words:

Pas Souillac—Digne.

Not Souillac, Dawlish said to himself, but Digne. He felt his heart beating faster at the realization of the significance of this. Macklin had been heading for Souillac, so this could only be a message for him. It did not matter that he might have killed Monet to make sure that Monet could not say where he had gone ; the only thing that mattered was to get after him.

And he must send for a doctor.

If anyone knew that he had been here he would be held for questioning, and that might take hours, could even take days. Not all French police would be as amiable as Corot or the grey-haired man of Auxerre. Now Dawlish began to feel under the pressure, the need for hurried departure. He stepped to the door, and all the consequences of being found on these premises with a dying man seemed to press upon him. How should he send for the doctor?

There was the obvious way, really the only way.

He lifted the telephone, and seemed to have to wait for an age before a man answered him. He said in his most fluent French: 'Send a doctor at once, please, to Monet & Cie, near the Grande Place,' and when the man said, 'Repeat that, please,' he repeated, 'Monet et Cie, near the Grande Place,' and then rang off. The telephone operator would almost certainly get in touch with the police, and if they moved as quickly as they had in Auxerre, he had only a few minutes to spare. He hurried down the stairs, no longer worried about making a little noise, and turned into the shop. He strode through it, pulled back two bolts, turned the knob of the lock and took away the chain. Then he opened the door quickly, stepped outside, and closed it without a click.

No one was in the square, but he heard the sound of a car engine. Could the police have been as quick as that? He stepped towards the hotel, hoping that the porter would not be there, and there was no need to worry. Only Felicity was in the doorway, and she came out as he approached.

'All right?'

'Let's get away in a hurry,' Dawlish said.

'What happened?'

'Someone else got to Monet before I did.'

'No,' Felicity said, in a strangled voice.

'Yes,' said Dawlish. 'But there was a note near the telephone.' He told her what he had read, what he felt sure was the truth. 'The chief worry is that the devil's probably changed cars again; it's no use hunting for the old Renault. We've got to pass 'em and recognize them.'

Felicity said, hopelessly, 'There just isn't a chance.'

'If you'd seen Monet you would say that we have to make a chance,' Dawlish said grimly. He took her arm and shepherded her across the road. The bright light seemed almost cruel in this silence. Then, as he got into the Lagonda, he heard the harsh beat of an engine, and felt sure that this was a police car, on the way to Monet's. If it reached the square before he left, the car would probably be stopped. The engine was so near that he knew he hadn't a chance of getting away before it arrived, and the only hope was to sit in the car; it would look as if it were empty from across the square.

A big car swung round a corner and headed for Monet's; and as it came to a standstill, brakes squealing, a clock boomed midnight and the lights in the square went out.

17

First Alarm

FELICITY exclaimed when the darkness fell upon them. There were only the twin orbs of the car which had just swung round the corner, and these leapt towards them, then swung towards the left. Dawlish actually chuckled. The roaring of the police car's engine was so loud that there was no danger of his self-starter being heard. The engine started at the first touch and he reversed, then swung across the dark square.

'But you can't see,' Felicity protested.

'You be my eyes,' Dawlish answered. 'That's a police wagon and we don't want to spend the night answering questions.' He shot the Lagonda forward at an alarming speed, and a lamp post loomed up.

'Mind!' cried Felicity.

'Your nerves aren't so good,' said Dawlish. He swung the wheel, then headed for the wide street opposite Monet's and away from the police car. Soon they were so used to the starlight that they could make out the shapes of the houses, some of them painted white or pale colours, and Felicity sat more at ease. Dawlish turned the first wide corner and then pulled into the side of the road and put on the side-lights.

'Better?'

'I'm all right,' Felicity said. 'But what point is there in running away from the police?'

'Monet was nearly dead and I could have attacked him—I trampled all over the place like a cart-horse. He'd obviously received a message for Macklin, which is in my pocket. Macklin isn't going to Souillac; he's on the way to Digne.'

'You mean where they have the thermal baths?'

'That's right,' agreed Dawlish. 'It's in the foothills of the French Alps. A nice place for murder, those particular mountains. Ivy Marshall was found in them.'

Felicity caught her breath. 'Then the police——'

'I shall telephone Corot as soon as I can and leave him to arrange a watch, but Macklin will almost certainly be in a different car, and it's almost certain that he isn't using his own name. It isn't going to be easy. I—oh, hell!'

'What's the matter?'

'I meant to check the signatures at the hotel. Five hundred francs would have got the forms out of that night porter,' Dawlish said bitterly. 'I didn't expect to leave in such a hurry. Tired, sweet?'

'I'm all right,' Felicity said, then asked in a quiet voice, 'Pat, what chance do you think there is of finding them before anything happens to the girl?'

'I'd put it at fifty-fifty if we hurry,' Dawlish answered. 'Now we've got to find the road to Clermont.' His torch shone straight and steady on to the map of Bourges. 'Hm . . . if we're where I think we are, we go straight across here, over the bridge, left on the other side, and then follow the river for a bit. It'll be as slow as a crawl, but at least there shouldn't be much on the road. Right, sweet?'

'Right,' said Felicity.

. . . . .

In Fontainebleau, M. Corot was talking on the telephone to the Inspector in Charge at Bourges. The Bourges inspector was a patient man, whereas Corot was most impatient; there was tension between them as the Bourges man said:

'There is no one of the name of Macklin at any hotel in Bourges, nor has there been anyone of that name. There is no Renault of the 1938 model registered at Cher parked in any of the parking places or in the garage of any hotel.

These things I tell you without hesitation or question. The man Monet'—Corot could almost imagine the way the other shrugged his shoulders—'even I cannot talk to a dead man. There is nothing to assist us, M. Corot. The big Englishman, Dawlish, was at the Hotel de la Poste for a short while, that is all. We are unable to find out which way he drove when he left the hotel. We have, however, reason to believe that he was in the shop of M. Monet, and we have arranged for a watch to be kept on the roads and for M. Dawlish to be stopped if——'

'No, no, no!' exclaimed Corot. 'Do not stop him whatever you do.'

'It is essential!'

'But if he killed M. Monet, which is unlikely, we can arrest him before they leave the country,' Corot argued. 'He is the easiest man to identify at the Customs barriers. If he did not, he may have seen Monet before Monet died, and might have reason to know which way Macklin went. I beg you, do not arrest M. Dawlish.'

'I shall refer the matter to *M. le Prefect* in the morning,' the Bourges man declared coldly.

'Do that,' said Corot resignedly. 'Have you searched the premises of M. Monet?'

'Yes.'

'What did you find there?'

'Much old furniture, some of it repaired very skilfully,' answered the Bourges inspector, 'and in the hollow legs of some of the chairs and tables, containers for cocaine. Some were empty, but . . .'

Corot could imagine him shrugging his shoulders again.

'I implore you to remember one thing,' said Corot fervently. 'It was Dawlish who first discovered such hiding places. If you wish to obtain approbation, you will go to other antique dealers in Bourges and nearby and find out if any of them have chairs and tables with hollow legs, and also find out where they have shipped repaired articles of furniture in the past few months. I think we shall find that the results of these inquiries are very interesting. Already in Fontainebleau and Auxerre five dealers have been discovered, some of them in possession of the drugs. And in each district there is an increase in drug addiction, known for some months. Is that a coincidence?'

He talked for five minutes, rang off, pushed his fingers through his sparse black hair, stared at the darkness of the street outside his window, and shook his head.

'I would like to know where Dawlish is,' he said quietly. 'And I would also like to know where that Kelvedon girl is.' He picked up a photograph of the boy who had been run down and killed, shook his head again, then looked at the photographs of the three men who had been captured at Auxerre. His eyes brightened. 'I think we shall soon have results of great importance,' he told the empty room. 'But whether the girl will survive . . .'

He shrugged, yawned, got up, put out the light, and went down the stairs and out to his small apartement near the police station.

• • • • •

Gillian pretended to be asleep.

She had been awake, in fact, for a long time, and she was stiff and cramped, yet dared move her body only a little, or Clive would know that she was awake; for the time being she did not want him to. She was surprised that she had slept at all, because her mind had been so full of uncertainties and clouded by vague fears.

She was very wide awake.

She was going over everything that there had been between them from the time of their first meeting. She could remember that vividly: how first his looks and then the way he had talked to her, had impressed her; and before the evening was out she had realized that he meant more to her than any other man she had ever known.

Why?

She could see that he had exerted some kind of fascination, and until a few hours ago she had been a willing victim of it. Now she was haunted by that uneasy sense of fear; the suspicion that he was in fact running away from the police, although he had scoffed at the idea and had given an explanation which had seemed reasonable. She had been greatly relieved at first, but now that there had been time to think she found herself wondering again, and wondering more than she had before.

From the beginning, Clive had wanted the marriage to be in secret. From the beginning he had wanted to bring her here, to France. The first day or two in Paris had been blissful, although he had been forced to leave her on her own more than she had expected, and once or twice when he had come back from a business appointment he had seemed subdued and a little on edge. But he had not allowed that to affect the way he talked to her, and she had not given it very much thought. Now she found herself thinking about every detail. The way they had driven to Auxerre, the changed car, the excuses about the car at Bourges, the fact that he had been out on his own, making calls which might be called furtive—all these things pressed themselves on her mind and she could not explain them.

Was it reasonable that a man with a splitting headache would want to drive through the night? She had been so concerned for him when he had first told her about his headache, but—was his edginess and his tension due to pain or fear? He was driving at great speed, as if there was some kind of fear that someone was on their heels?

What kind of trouble was he in?

How much had he lied to her?

She had a little shivery feeling at the thought that he might have deceived her, then told herself that she couldn't be right about that, it was absurd. He had seemed so honest about their whole relationship, and there was no doubt that he had taken her to the mayor's house, that the mayor had married them.

Or—could there be anything wrong, even with that?

She eased herself up a little and opened her eyes a crack, to look at him. She was surprised that dawn was breaking.

She could see him very much more clearly than she had half-an-hour ago. His profile was handsome beyond words. He sat more relaxed than she had seen him for some time. His body was relaxed, too, as if he was no longer under pressure; perhaps his head no longer ached.

He glanced at her.

'Hallo!' He gave his quick, glowing smile. 'Awake?'

She answered in a yawny voice, to make him think that she had just woken.

'Soon will be.'

'You look just as beautiful there as if we were where we ought to be,' he declared, and took his eyes off the road for what seemed to be a dangerously long time.

Gillian sat up slowly.

'How's your head, darling?'

'Clear as a bell. The driving worked, you see.'

'That's good.'

'Hungry?'

'I suppose I am, rather, but I haven't had time to think about it,' Gillian answered. 'I'll have to spend a penny before long.'

'In twenty minutes we should be in a town called Macon. We'll stop at a hotel there, and wash and brush up and eat a hearty breakfast before we hit the road again. Might as well make all the mileage while we can. The country's pretty dull until we get into the mountains down south.'

'How far have we come?' Gillian asked.

'Getting on for two hundred miles,' Macklin answered. 'One of the fastest runs I've ever done—and you slept like a top! Shows you have a clear conscience.'

Gillian retorted, almost before she realized what she was saying:

'Of course I have. Haven't you?'

She saw the way his expression changed, how his eyes narrowed for a moment, and she thought that he would shout at her; but he did not, and in fact he forced a grin.

'Couldn't be clearer,' he declared, and looked ahead of him. 'Ah, here's a straight stretch, we should really be able to make this thing move along here.' He put his foot down hard on the accelerator, and the car seemed to fly over the narrow road.

Gillian watched him intently.

18

Questions

'CLIVE.'

'Yes, honey?'

'Can you slow down for a minute.'

'But why? It's the best road we've had all the morning.'

'Just for a minute.'

'Right-ho,' Macklin conceded, and eased his foot off the accelerator. 'Tired?'

'Not really, but you must be,' Gillian said. 'You've been driving hard since we left Macon at eight o'clock, and it's now nearly twelve.'

'Well, we had a good breakfast, didn't we?'

'It's silly to overdo it.'

'The quicker the journey's over and the business done, the sooner we'll be in our room overlooking the Mediterranean, and let me tell you, that's going to be really something!'

'Is it, darling?'

'Doubt it?'

'Clive,' asked Gillian quietly, 'what are you running away from?'

She saw the way he gripped the wheel, making the car swerve, and knew beyond all doubt that he hated the question and that it had shocked him. He stared straight ahead after a first moment of surprise, and it was some time before he answered:

'Don't talk nonsense.'

'Is it nonsense, Clive?'

'What the hell do you think I'm running away from?'

'I don't know,' Gillian said. 'I only know——'

'You're talking out of the back of your neck. Good God, what a thing to suggest—that I'm running away. What do you think I've got to run away from? Another wife, tucked in the background? *I'm* not a bigamist!'

'Clive, I didn't mean——'

'You seem to think I've got some guilty secret. Come on, let's hear about it,' Clive rasped. He swung off the road between two trees, so fast that the car lurched to and fro, and it looked as if he would bang into one of the trees; he stopped within inches of it, jammed on the brake, and then swung round in his seat to face her. His face was very pale, and his eyes glittered; he was much more tired than he had admitted. There was tension at his mouth, too, and it drew the lips tight at the corners, spoiling his good looks.

'Clive, please. . . .'

'Now come on. Out with it. What guilty secret do you think I've got?' he demanded, and glared at her. 'It's time we had this out.'

'Clive, I only——'

'Come on, out with it!'

Gillian thought, with a flash of intuition, 'He's frightened of me now.'

Her heart was beating very fast, but no longer with excitement. She heard the whine of an approaching car and glanced at it, almost wishing that it would stop, but it hurtled by. In the distance a huge truck was coming towards them, spewing dark exhaust into the air above it, but apart from that there were only the fields and the distant clouds and the clear blue sky above them, with the sun burning down through the sparse foliage of the trees above their heads.

'Are you going to tell me, or aren't you?' he demanded, and he gripped her wrist.

'Clive,' Gillian said, 'if you're in any kind of trouble I want to help.'

'What the devil do you mean, any kind of trouble? Come on, tell me—what's on your mind?'

'It isn't any use shouting at me,' Gillian said. 'It's just that you seem as if you're running away all the time, and——'

'That's a lie! You've got a run-away complex, just because you eloped. I suppose the truth is that you regret it. You wish you'd stuck in London, and waited for your precious mother, so that she can dominate your future in the same way that she's dominated your past.'

Gillian said sharply, 'We'll leave my mother out of this.'

'We'll talk about her or anyone else I like, and I want to know——'

Gillian wrenched her hand free, used the other hand to open the door, and as it swung open, she slid out. She felt Clive grab at her and his nails bite into her wrist, but she drew herself free and stood by the side of the car. A fresh wind helped to minimise the fierce heat of the sun. Beyond the shadow of the trees even the green looked harsh and hot, and there was a kind of shimmer which hurt her eyes, perhaps because she had slept so little. She stalked away from the car, her lips set tightly, her eyes bright and glittering. She had never felt so angry and so bitter. If he came after her, if he touched her, she would strike him. She heard him coming. The stubble of the field beyond looked thick and uncomfortable to walk on, and she had only light shoes. There was a shallow dip in the land between the verge and the stubble, and she reached this and turned towards the right, away from the direction in which they had been going.

He hadn't called out after her.

He *was* frightened.

He was just behind her, and spoke stiffly: 'Are you going to answer my question, or aren't you? What do you think I am running away from?'

She hesitated, and then turned round to face him—and she was startled by what she saw. His eyes were glassy and glittering, and his mouth was still drawn tightly across his teeth, giving him that almost ugly look. His hands were raised a little in front of him, the fingers crooked. He hardly seemed the Clive whom she knew so well, whom she loved, whom——

Whom she hardly knew at all.

The great truck came labouring up, the engine roaring

and the road shaking beneath it. Smoke now poured out of the exhaust which pointed towards the sky, and the stink of the diesel oil was pungent in Gillian's nostrils, and yet she hardly noticed that. She stood with her back against a tree, staring at Clive, her heart thumping painfully, her eyes almost as bright as his. She found her hands clenching, too. She realized that this was what she had often heard about and laughed about: a first quarrel.

'Clive, I've told you that if you're in any trouble, I want to help you,' she managed to say calmly. 'Don't let's quarrel, it will spoil everything if we do.'

'I'd like to know who started it.'

'I don't know who started it and I don't care,' Gillian retorted. Her own temper was on a tight leash, and if she lost it completely nothing would prevent this from becoming a savage quarrel; only too obviously Clive had just as vile a temper. Yet she hated the thought of quarrelling, for she felt a kind of compassion for him, who had been so strong, and was now showing how weak he could be. He looked tired to a point of collapse—it would be easy to believe now that he had a pounding headache; and yet a few minutes before he had seemed so much better. He opened his mouth to speak again, and somehow she felt that she had to prevent him, that if he shouted or spoke roughly she would not be able to control herself. 'Clive!' she said, quite sharply. 'We can't stand here in the middle of France quarrelling like two children. I'm sorry if I upset you. I thought you were worried about something, and I wanted to help. After all, I'm not completely blind. You have been behaving strangely since we left Paris. We never stay long in the same place, and you've changed the car twice. There isn't anything remarkable about my wondering why, is there?'

He stared at her for what seemed a very long time, until he said hoarsely:

'No. No, I see what you mean. I'm sorry.'

'It doesn't matter, Clive. I only want to help.'

'I don't think you can.'

'There is something worrying you, isn't there?' Gillian

demanded. 'Ever since we left Paris you've had something on your mind. Why don't you tell me what it is? I might be able to help much more than you think.'

He stood staring across at the distant clouds, as if wishing them nearer. Yet they seemed further away, and the sky above was burnished. Two more great trucks rumbled and clattered past, then two cars raced each other and swished by; after that the road and the fields were empty, and they were utterly alone.

• • • • •

Macklin thought: I could finish her off now.

Gillian was standing with her back against a slender poplar, and she would not be able to get away from him. She was pleading with him, and reasoning, but he hardly knew what she was saying, his fear was so great. Obviously she had deep suspicions—and Sharp had been absolutely right. She was dangerous; if she got away she could become deadly.

There was this shallow ditch. He could cover the body with stubble.

That was crazy! It would be fatal, deadly. A dozen motorists might stop here, and the body could be found within a few minutes—certainly within an hour or two. There would have to be somewhere to conceal the body for forty-eight hours, remember. And for the time being he must placate her. What had she said? 'I might be able to help you more than you think.' Help! He could have laughed in her face, but he did not; instead he fought to keep the fear and the anger out of his expression. He must satisfy her with a plausible explanation, and one thing was now certain: he must admit that he had some cause for being upset. For being frightened, too? No, he mustn't admit that he was frightened or running away. He must think of some convincing reason to explain the changed cars, the haste, the fact that he had been so much on edge. Oh, God, why couldn't he think of something? And why did she stand there so still and upright, her body so beautiful, her bare arms so rounded and slender? Oh, God, why had this had to happen?

Think of something.

There was such transparent honesty in her eyes. He had a strange feeling that she could see through him, and that she knew that whatever he said would be a lie. He must be absolutely convincing, just needed some simple and straightforward explanation.

He moistened his lips, and turned away to look at those distant clouds, a little more than a line of cotton wool on the horizon. Then an old man came trudging along the road, carrying a long pitchfork over his shoulder, wearing ragged clothes and thick heavy boots, and carrying a red cloth filled with food. A wine bottle stuck out of his pocket as he lumbered past, and he glanced at them and gave an almost nervous nod.

'*M'sieu—'dame.*'

'*M'sieu,*' Macklin said. He was glad of the moment's respite while he told himself what a lunatic he had nearly been; even the open fields concealed people, there might be a dozen watching them now. If he had lost his self-control and attacked Gillian then, he wouldn't have got as far as the next village.

Gillian was still silent in an accusing kind of way, and he still had to satisfy her.

He must appeal to her sympathy—to her womanly understanding. He must be very cautious and gentle, because he had to make sure that she stayed with him: he would be the one to decide when they were to part, and if her temper was anything to judge by, she was capable of flaring up and going off on her own.

'Clive——' she began.

'All right, Gillian,' Macklin said very quietly. 'I suppose I shouldn't have tried to keep it to myself, but there is something worrying me. It started in Paris, too.' He gulped and moistened his lips, and prayed that she did not think that this indicated that he was lying. 'It's about the job.'

Her expression changed on the instance.

'The job?' She sounded almost pleased.

'Yes,' he answered, and hoped that he sounded miserable enough. 'There was a message waiting for me in Paris. Apparently someone from another firm is on the same hunt as I am, for some very special pieces of French furniture, and I lost one or two to this other chap. I was told that unless I could recoup my losses, so to speak, I would soon be looking for another job. And—well, to happen just now, when we've only been married a few days . . .'

Gillian's face began to glow again, the change was quite remarkable.

'Darling, why didn't you tell me! If *that's* all . . .'

'All!'

'You wouldn't be the first man who had to look for another job!'

'But coming just now, it's dreadful,' Macklin declared, hardly able to believe that he had been so successful; but the radiance of her eyes convinced him that he had. 'And to make it worse, this other chap's ahead of me all the way. When the Jag broke down at Auxerre I was beside myself, but I didn't want to spoil things for you, and I took the first car I could get. But speed counts, darling. I've got to get to the town of Digne, and then to Nice and Cannes, ahead of this chap. If he reaches the customers before me, then . . .' Macklin shrugged, and then held out his right hand and jerked the thumb towards the ground. 'I just had to get a better car. It must have looked peculiar, but I had to do it through acquaintances on the road. I haven't enough cash to buy one, and no one will hire one out to a stranger. That's why——'

Gillian threw herself into his arms.

• • • • •

'You ought to have a few hours rest,' Gillian urged when they got back into the car. 'It won't be any use if you're exhausted when you get to Digne. How far ahead is this man?'

'About a day, as far as I can judge. He was at Bourges

yesterday morning. By driving through the night we've gained the better part of a day. With luck we'll catch up with him at Grenoble.'

'Can't you rest just for an hour or two?'

'I shouldn't.'

'Why don't you take a chance and let me drive, while you close your eyes,' said Gillian. 'I can't drive so fast as you and I've never driven on this side of the road before, but——'

'That's a wonderful idea!' Macklin applauded. 'And the road couldn't be much straighter here. Take over, darling!'

He thought, as they got out of the car: "It's all right, there's nothing to worry about. I fooled her." This was the first time that he was completely dispassionate about her, but he gave that hardly a thought. He had overcome his "love"; he saw the danger she could be to him, now, and he simply had to obey Sharp.

It was just a question of time and place.

Gillian drove at about fifty miles an hour, fast enough to make him feel that they were making progress, and steadily enough for him to lean back and close his eyes: it was not until he did so that he realized how tired he was. His eyes would not open, even when he wanted them to. There was sufficient wind coming in at the windows to keep him cool, but not to keep him awake. The hum of the tyres on the hard road lulled him to sleep. He heard Gillian change gear, and felt the car turn out and then pass a farm cart; she could drive quite well: she could drive herself to death! His lips curved.

He hardly gave the future a thought.

Sleep was wonderful.

He wondered what old Sharp was doing in that little office in the Strand; or else in the hotel in Paris, where he had last come to talk. Sharp didn't really like Paris, for some reason or another. Smart chap, Sharp! He had organized the whole set-up from the beginning, and it had been running for years: a European-wide sales organization for antique furniture using some of the pieces to convey drugs, medicines, tobacco, and jewels, from places where they were stolen or smuggled, to the main distributing centres, mostly in big cities.

It was too big an organization to risk for one girl's sake.

What was that?

He heard Gillian, singing softly to herself.

. . . . .

It was in a little town halfway to Grenoble that Macklin saw newspapers hanging outside a shop near the hotel where they went for a meal, that he saw the headline about the murder of Monet.

'My God,' he thought, 'Sharp meant to make sure no one knew where I was heading. Sharp's smart all right!' He pretended to look at the headlines while waiting for Gillian, whose eye had been attracted by some *pâtisserie* in a small shop nearby. When she came out, he was smiling and gay, and he made no comment on Monet's murder. But his thoughts were racing because of it. He felt quite sure that Sharp had laid it on simply to make sure that he, Macklin, could not be traced. Certainly the police weren't after him, or he would have known by now, even if Dawlish had put them on to him; the switching of cars and names had put them off the scent, and put Dawlish off, too.

He could take a little more time.

They ought to be in the Basse Alpes by mid afternoon tomorrow, even if they slept at an hotel tonight—and they could both do with a night's sleep. By tomorrow it would be all over, and he would pick up Sharp's next message at Digne.

What a man to work for!

19

Sharp

THE small office overlooking the Strand was empty. The woman in the outer office was sitting at her typewriter and typing almost casually. In front of her were some invoices for pieces of furniture which to her were just wood and ornamentation, but which seemed to be worth a fortune. In the office there was a record of all the sales made by Sharp through his agents—and the main sales and buying agent was Clive Macklin.

She smiled at the thought of Macklin. There was a man who really had the looks.

She heard the lift stop at the landing and heard footsteps; she felt sure they were Sharp's. He pushed open the door, and she saw a little Frenchman behind him, named Rougemont; she had always thought that it was too fine-sounding a name for an insignificant little man. Sharp nodded to her, and Rougemont bowed, before they went into the inner office. She heard the key turn in the lock. Sharp always made sure that she could not burst in when he was really anxious not to be overheard. She suspected that some of the furniture that he sold was faked, and that he was determined to keep it to himself. Her typing quickened a little; she had long since stopped being really curious about what went on in the other office.

In there, Sharp was sitting behind the small desk, his polished, manicured nails touching lightly as he held his fingers together. His French was fluent as his English, and he listened attentively. The only other sound was the hum of traffic from the Strand and the tapping of the typewriter keys.

Rougemont finished. He was a handsome little man with

jet black hair and a pronounced widow's peak, and he dressed with the same kind of finicky care as Sharp.

Sharp said, 'Yes, I agree, it was necessary to kill Monet. Are you now sure that this man Dawlish is not on the road to Souillac?'

'Quite certain,' Rougemont said.

'And he is heading for the Riviera?'

'Beyond question.'

'Is there no indication that the police are after Macklin?'

'It has not been reported,' said Rougemont. 'I have telephoned all of our agents *en route* and they have watched for the English car and Dawlish and his wife—there is no doubt about them. And they have also watched for Macklin and his new wife in the car which he hired through Monet.'

'How far ahead is Macklin?'

'Perhaps half a day.'

Sharp picked up a silver pencil and rolled it round and round between the soft, pale palms.

'No more?'

'It is not long enough,' Rougemont said. 'The Lagonda is a faster car.'

'Yes. And Macklin will undoubtedly go off the main road before he gets to Digne, and attempt to kill the girl there.'

'It is the obvious place.'

'Yes,' agreed Sharp. 'Yes. If Dawlish should catch up with them before the girl is dead——'

'He must not, *m'sieu.*'

'No, he must not,' agreed Sharp. 'Do you mean that he will not?'

'There will be a slight accident.' Rougemont shrugged. 'I cannot guarantee that he will be killed, but he will be delayed quite long enough. *M'sieu* . . .'

'Yes?'

'How important to you is this Macklin?'

Sharp began to smile a little. He had rather full, very well-shaped lips, almost like the lips of a voluptuous woman. His eyes had long lashes, too, and were so brilliant that it looked as if he used a little eye shade, to help them. There was something quite feminine about him; and at that moment, something feline.

'He is not important now,' he said. 'He was, but—the police are bound to get him, soon. Don't you agree?'

'Absolutely, *m'sieu*!' Rougemont looked as if he were delighted. 'Then what do you propose?'

'I propose that you should make sure that Macklin and the girl die together—or at least, that Macklin dies very soon after the girl, so that no one can question him.' Sharp was pursing his lips in a smile which looked one of real amusement. 'Macklin collects our goods from how many shops?'

'Twenty-one, *m'sieu.*'

'Ah, yes,' mused Sharp. 'I knew it was twenty-one or two. After this he will never get safely out of France, so that he must be killed goes without saying. The task is to make sure that he cannot lead to anyone else. Those we have lost, we have lost, but they knew only the contacts Macklin had. If the worst comes to the worst and the whole of that side of the organization has to be closed, what is it?'

'One shop in five, *m'sieu.*'

'Yes. And as each shopkeeper will get rid of any goods immediately—you have sent them word?'

'Of course, *m'sieu.*'

'Then it does not matter greatly if the police talk to every one of the twenty-one shops,' Sharp said, 'for every shopkeeper will deny any knowledge of illicit goods, and the police will find nothing if they search. Am I right?'

'In every way,' Rougemont approved.

'So it is just a matter of making sure that Dawlish does not catch up with Macklin until Macklin and his wife are dead,' said Sharp. 'Can you arrange it?'

'It is arranged, except that I have to give the order,' Rougemont assured him. 'That is why I flew over this morning. I did not want to go further than I had without consulting you.'

'I don't usually like any decisions being taken without

my approval,' Sharp said, 'but this time you were right.' His smile broadened and he showed his white teeth for a moment. 'Good. Do you have a telephone?'

'I shall telephone Paris from here if that is permitted,' said Rougemont. 'Our friend in Paris will telephone Grenoble, and our friend in Grenoble will telephone Digne. That is the safest way, I think.'

'Use that telephone,' Sharp said. 'Provided only that you don't say anything to incriminate me!'

He gave a little soft chuckle as Rougemont leaned forward for a telephone which had a direct line to the exchange, and gave a Paris number.

. . . . .

'Goodness!' Felicity exclaimed, several hundred miles away from London. 'It's hot!'

'I thought you liked heat,' Dawlish remarked lazily.

'This is abnormal.'

'Oh, no more than ninety or so in the shade.'

'That's if there were any shade.'

'Will be, soon,' Dawlish assured her. 'When we're a bit further on we'll run through wooded land in the climb up to the mountains. Like to pull off the road for half an hour?'

'I'd rather keep going,' said Felicity.

She knew that he would have hated stopping, and she meant it when she said she would rather go on. In one way she had never been so much on edge as she was now, and the worst part about the situation was that they had to go on driving blindly, not even being absolutely sure that their quarry was ahead. They had stopped three times at police stations, after Dawlish had talked to Corot of Fontainebleau the previous afternoon, and the police had no information for them. It was now known that Macklin had used the name of Lane at two hotels, and carried documents under that name; he might have other *aliases*, too. No one knew what car he was using, and France was littered with English touring couples. Every hotel on the known routes was being watched and all registrations scrutinized, but there was no certainty that Macklin had stopped overnight at any hotel.

Felicity said, 'I suppose they might even be on the Riviera by now.'

'Could be.'

'Pat . . .'

'Hm-hm?'

'Is it really worth going on?'

He glanced at her and said, 'I'd hate to go back and talk to Mrs. Kelvedon and tell her that we gave up because we weren't sure which road they'd taken.'

Very slowly Felicity nodded.

The heat seemed to be carried into the car on the wind; it was not really cool with the windows right down. There was a haze everywhere. Whenever she took off her sunglasses she had to close her eyes, the light was so strong and vicious. Dawlish drove with his eyes narrowed all the time: he disliked sunglasses, but now she thought that his eyes were watering a little, and that sooner or later he would have to put them on; today, especially, he wanted to be able to see everything with crystal clarity. She saw that he watched the driving mirror, and that whenever they passed a car parked at the side of the road he glanced at it as if making a mental note of the number. All the time his mind was alert, and he was trying to make sure that he did not miss a thing which might help them to find Gillian; but she felt a sense of acute depression, for she did not think there was any real chance at all.

But he was right to go on.

They flashed by one of the newest model Citroens, and Dawlish studied it, and studied the man and woman standing by the side of it, each holding a long piece of golden brown bread and a plate of what looked like *paté*. The car was a pale grey. She saw Dawlish watching the mirror very closely for the next five minutes, and although he did not say a word she sensed that something had happened to quicken his attention.

'What is it?' Felicity asked.

'Remember that Citroen?'
'The grey one with the fair-haired woman by it?'
'Yes.'
'What about it? Is it coming up?'
'Fast,' said Dawlish.
'You know how fast those Citroens are, and——'
'Remember that they were eating?' asked Dawlish, quietly. 'They had half a long loaf each, and some *paté*. They must have stopped eating the moment we were out of sight and come after us.'
Felicity felt a tightness at her throat.
'I see,' she said.
'And they must have taken it for granted that we wouldn't guess they were interested in us,' Dawlish guessed. 'Sit so that you can grab the arm and the strap, if I should have to stop in a hurry. I don't want you to crash your head on the windscreen.'
Felicity said huskily, 'I'm ready.' She leaned forward so that she could see the Citroen, and her heart lurched because it was so near.

20

Tactics

'How far behind is it now?' asked Felicity.

'A hundred yards or so.'

'Is it getting nearer?'

'No—it's keeping its distance because of the curves in the road,' Dawlish said. 'Darling, if you were doing what I think they're going to try, where would you do it?'

'Don't make me think about it.'

'Someone has to.'

'Are we—are we going through some hills now?'

'Yes.'

'Then I'd try it on a curve.'

'That's right,' said Dawlish. 'And the route map says that there are some steep gradients and nasty bends. Nice view, isn't it?'

'What will you do?'

'Wait and watch,' Dawlish answered.

'The other driver probably knows the road better than you do.'

'His car's more manoeuvrable, too,' said Dawlish cheerlessly, and there was hardness in his eyes when he glanced down at her. 'It'll be all right, sweet. He can't do any harm, as we're expecting him to try. If he'd caught us by surprise——'

He frowned.

'What is it, Pat?'

Dawlish didn't answer, but his frown brought a furrow between his eyebrows, and he thrust his chin forward as if he were facing some new and unpleasant thought. There was a great deal of light-coloured stone and rock down the hillsides, and the glare off them was dazzling; that might be one of the things that was making him frown. She wished he would answer, but did not want to nag him; he must be thinking with almost desperate anxiety.

Then he said, 'They've been good, haven't they? I mean, good in the sense of efficient.'

'I suppose so.'

'Brilliant, in their way,' Dawlish went on. 'And this car's been on our tail for how long?'

'Twenty minutes.'

'How many chances have they missed?'

'Several, I suppose.'

'Very good chances,' said Dawlish, 'and they've positively thrown them away. Yet these people don't throw much away. What would you think was the explanation?'

'Pat, concentrate; don't talk.'

'Sometimes it's better to think aloud, you might even have a bright idea,' Dawlish said, and glanced down at her and grinned. 'They're not after us, Fel.'

'*What?*'

'The key to pushing us off the road is surprise,' Dawlish said. 'They probably know I've a bit of a reputation, and they'll try to out-think us.'

'Us!'

'That's right,' agreed Dawlish, but he was not really thinking about what he was saying. He was watching the road ahead as often as he was looking in the driving mirror. Felicity did not attempt to understand, or attempt to stop him from talking. 'They're acting as the pacemaker.'

'The what?'

'Pacemaker. They're setting the pace,' went on Dawlish with great care. 'They know that we're on the look-out for something like this. They must know that we've been watching them in the mirror all the time. They've had a dozen chances to pass and haven't taken one. Their job is to keep us on edge, and so make it easier when the real attempt starts.'

'Real——' Felicity began, and then went on: 'You think they'll use another car?'

'Yes. Coming downhill. Much easier to push us off the road if a car comes downhill at us when we're not expecting it,' went on Dawlish, still speaking with great deliberation. 'I expect something to come hurtling down soon, but not until the chaps behind have signalled.' He began to smile rather tensely, 'They'll have to signal by blowing their horn very loudly, or by waving.' He changed gear to take a nasty bend, and Felicity held her breath, but no car lurked behind it. She looked back at the other car every time they turned a corner. She had not realized how far they had climbed, nor how long a drop there was. Way below them stretched the winding road; all about them were the pale rocks and the stunted trees.

The heat seemed to burn down at her, and her eyes were smarting badly. Dawlish's face seemed set more grimly than ever, but there was a glint in his eyes which told that, in a way, he was enjoying this.

Then he exclaimed: 'Look!'

One of the people in the car behind was waving a handkerchief or a duster out of the window. It was done very casually and easily—as anyone might shake a duster. It was the woman, and she took her time. Felicity glanced up and saw a car perched on the side of the road, two bends above them. She felt her heart beating painfully fast. Dawlish was smiling very broadly, but it was a set smile. He swung round a corner faster than he had any of the others, and as he did so, Felicity saw a cloud of dust where the other car had been; the car itself was hidden by the mountain side. She looked down. The valley below was thickly wooded, but the sun seemed to shimmer off the rocks and off the tiny streams below. Felicity clenched the arm of her seat and the strap by her door. Dawlish took another corner more slowly and widely. Felicity realized that at the next one the other car was likely to swing round.

She clenched her hands, and was clenching her teeth so tightly that her jaws hurt. The first car was out of sight, but she had forgotten it, she was so sure that Pat was right.

'Here it comes,' he warned.

She did not know whether he heard it, or whether he heard some sign of movement. The road ahead was fairly wide, but there had been a fall of rocks, and some of the cliff had fallen, leaving a patch of rubble. Near the corner the road narrowed so that there was barely room for two cars to pass. Felicity felt like screaming because Pat took everything so calmly. He pulled in close to the side of the cliff, tyres crunching over the rubble of rock, and a cloud of white dust arose. He put on the brake, stopped, and opened the door in what seemed like the same movement, and before she realized what he meant to do, he was striding towards the corner, where at any second she expected the other car to appear.

'Pat, come back!'

He actually glanced round and waved at her, and she saw the automatic in his hand. Then the nose of the car appeared at the corner, and the grinding and squealing of brakes was hideous. Small rocks and stones were being pushed over the edge, and she heard them rattling down. The dust was thicker near the corner, and she expected the whole car to swing round the corner. Instead, it stopped so that only the long nose of a Renault appeared.

Felicity began to run after Pat.

She glanced down and saw the grey Citroen, at least three bends in the road below. It was stopped by the edge. The man was standing by the open door and the woman was getting out; they stared as if they could not believe what they were seeing. They looked absurdly far away, pigmy figures a long way off and dwarfed by the great hills and the huge rocks and the tall trees.

Dawlish reached the corner and stood to one side, peering round. Felicity heard a grating sound, strangely loud in the near silence. A long way off, rubble was still falling. From somewhere above their heads came the sound of another engine. She began to run. Then she heard the sharp sound of a shot near the corner and saw a spurt of dust as a bullet struck the rock of the cliff five yards away from Pat's head. He ventured round the wall of rock, and his right hand was hidden from her; in it was his gun. She saw his elbow go back, as if he were taking aim.

There was a sharp report.

She thought there was a cry, and then there were scrabbling sounds, as of someone running. Pat was actually grinning. She reached his side, and he knew just where she was because he put out his left arm behind him, to stop her from going too close to the corner.

'Where is he?'

'Oh, he's running round the mountain, so he is,' Dawlish began to sing in a deep voice. 'Oh, he's running round the mountain, so he is. He's so scared you'd never believe it, if he's got a gun he'll never need it, so he's running round the mountain, so he is!' He swung towards her, and held her tightly as they rounded the corner and the nose of the other car.

Felicity saw a running figure a long way below.

It was the driver of the Renault racing down the side of the hills. His car was empty. A little billow of dust fell whenever the man's feet kicked against the chalky rocks. Dawlish was still smiling, but the edge of his excitement had gone, and he glanced down at the driver of the Citroen and the woman with him. They were still standing by their car.

'I shouldn't think they'll try to finish what he started,' Dawlish said dryly. 'But there's always a chance. Looks as if the Renault was there to force us off the edge when we reached the corner, in a nice little accident, but as we stopped the chap lost his head and used a gun. I wish I'd time to look for the bullet, but we ought to get a move on.' Felicity saw that he was perspiring although he was breathing quite evenly. 'We'd better clear this Renault off the road, then get to the top as fast as we can. Pity we couldn't catch the beggar,' he added, staring after the running man, who disappeared among some trees and was cut off from sight. 'He might possibly have some idea where Macklin and Gillian are. Hell of a business, isn't it?' He stepped to the back of the Renault, bent down, and gripped the flimsy bumper. 'Heave,' he said, half-jokingly, and raised the back of the car and swivelled it round several inches before putting it down. 'Once again—heave!'

'What are you trying to do?'

'Get it ready to roll over,' answered Dawlish simply. 'Heave!' The sweat was running down his face, but he had done what he wanted, and now stepped to the side of the car, opened the door and then took off the hand brake. He pushed, and the car began to roll forward. Felicity saw it lurch to one side, and heard a grating sound as it scraped on the edge of the road. She went forward, and put her weight against it, and Dawlish called: 'That's the spirit. Heave! . . . Look out!'

She darted back.

Dawlish was closer to the car as it toppled over, and it seemed to hang for a moment on the edge of the road, the near-side wheel in the air, the undercarriage gaping at her. Then he simply put the flat of his hand against one side, and the car toppled over and crashed down with a great rending noise and a huge cloud of dust.

'Let's go,' he said.

Felicity didn't say a word as she hurried back to the Lagonda. The two people were getting into the Citroen; they still seemed a long way below. Pat waved to them as he took the wheel. He reversed a few yards, and then drove forward, turned the corner, and said, 'Wipe my forehead for me, sweet, I can't see for sweat.' She took her handkerchief out of her bag, and in a moment it was wet through. 'One in my pocket,' went on Dawlish. Now that the strain was over and he was suffering from reaction he was driving more slowly; and Felicity knew that at the back of his mind there was the fear that someone else would be waiting for them, or that the Citroen would gain on them. She finished wiping his forehead. He turned two more sharp bends, and then came upon a longer, wider stretch of road; a huge lorry faced them. He had to pull close to the verge to get past.

'See if you can see the blonde,' Dawlish urged.

'I keep looking.'

'Any sign of the man who ran away?'

'No,' said Felicity. 'I—there's the Citroen!'

'Gaining?'

'It's going the other way.'

'Oh, no,' said Dawlish, and suddenly his smile seemed to be completely relaxed, as if fear had been taken away. 'So they couldn't take it, Fel. Sure it's the same one?'

'It's a pale grey Citroen, and we haven't passed one.'

'You're right, we haven't. Wave them goodbye!' Dawlish brushed the back of his hand across his forehead, which was damp again, and went on in a harder voice: 'It's still a question of whether we can find Gillian. I'd hoped we could catch the driver of the Renault, but he meant to make sure that we couldn't. He might have led us——' Dawlish broke off. 'Light me a cigarette, sweet.'

Felicity lit one, and he leaned sideways to take it between his lips.

'Thanks. One thing's certain.'

'What?'

'It's still like looking for a marked pebble on a beach, but if Gillian is alive . . .' he hesitated for what seemed a long time, and didn't go on.

21

Passport

'WONDERFUL road, isn't it?' Macklin asked.

'It's a bit frightening,' Gillian answered.

'Oh, it's as safe as houses.'

'I wouldn't like to drive along here myself,' Gillian told him.

'Scared?'

'Not really, but at some of the corners you go a bit fast.'

'You should see me when I'm driving without precious cargo,' Macklin said, and he gave a gust of laughter which startled her; there was a wild note about it. There had been moments when he had laughed, other moments since their quarrel when his voice had sharpened. For an hour or more she had been completely satisfied that he had told her the truth, but sitting there on the monotonous road, watching it stretching out in front of her, she had begun to ask herself more questions.

He had told her in London that his job with Sharps was absolutely safe, yet said that he had been told that it wasn't when he was in Paris. That had been the first sliver of doubt to enter her head, but others had quickly followed. Had he really behaved like a man setting out to catch up with a competitor and pass him? If so, he would surely have been looking ahead all the time; she was quite sure that he had been more worried about what lay behind. And would the threat of the loss of his job affect him like this trouble had? It might challenge him, it might make him eager, but would it really frighten him?

He had been frightened; she was quite sure of that.

Now and again she had looked at his sleeping form. He lay awkwardly back in his seat, his mouth very slack, quite different from the way it had looked when he had shouted at her. In the quiet of the drive, she found herself thinking more about that. He hadn't been normal, and had really frightened her. For a while she had been so anxious to find a satisfactory explanation that the story he had told her had seemed perfectly reasonable, but it did not explain the tautness of his nerves and the way he had talked to her.

What was the real trouble?

She began to think again—and to remember odd little things: for instance, at the hotels where they had stayed he had always sent her up to their room while he had signed the forms they used instead of a register in France. She had thought that was because he had wanted to save her any embarrassment because they had not been married before Auxerre. But was that a good explanation? Or had he wanted to keep anything from her?

The passports were in his briefcase, and that reminded her of another thing: he always carried the briefcase himself, and he always kept it locked. She had not given that much thought, but now the recollection of the way he had held it under his arm wherever they had gone had struck her as peculiar; he had taken it to the dining-room with them. She began to wonder why it was so important.

And there were the other things which she had noticed before, and which he had appeared to explain; but there was nothing really satisfactory about his explanation. She found it necessary to start thinking afresh and start worrying afresh. Was he normal? Even if normal, was he running away from someone? Or was he simply anxious to get to a certain place quickly?

She had kept on driving.

Now she remembered these things as he drove round the tortuous mountain bends. They had come through a town called Gap not long before, and he had told her that Digne was only forty miles away. He had seemed in high spirits after luncheon at a small wayside hotel where they had been the only customers, and he had rattled off his French as if he had been a native. The excitement was still in him. He was smiling all the time. Now and again he bared his teeth, as if he were getting ready for a fight. He was different from the Clive she had known in London; there was a kind of rawness about him. When he spoke to her now it was brusquely, almost offhandedly, as if she no longer mattered. The last time he had taken any trouble to ease her feelings had been after the quarrel.

Perhaps he was happier because this was near the end of the journey.

She had not been able to look inside the briefcase, but she had handled it and found it locked. He had not noticed her. Now she had one major preoccupation: to find out what was in the briefcase. But she did not think there was much hope.

It was scorching hot and Clive was perspiring freely, but it did not seem to worry him.

They turned a bend in the road and the view beyond looked even more beautiful than before. For a moment Gillian was captivated by the vastness of the mountain-tops spread all about them, and the beauty of the metallic-looking sky, and she almost forgot her fears.

Clive slowed down.

'Like to get out and have a stroll?' he suggested. 'I know a beautiful look-out point just off the road. There's a place to park, too.'

He was staring at her intently, and she realized that he wanted her to say yes. She did not understand why she did not like the thought. It was so odd: this seemed the last place in the world to get out and walk, and he had been in such a desperate hurry before. That was odd; since they had come upon these twisting roads he had driven without any sense of urgency, but he had seen no one except in her presence. So far as it was possible for her to judge, nothing had changed.

'I—I think it's too hot,' she said.

'This isn't hot,' he scoffed, and grinned. 'In North Africa it really gets scorching.'

'Have you been there?'

'Often,' he told her. 'That's quite a place. One of these days you'll have to come and see it.'

He laughed.

'He's *not* normal,' Gillian thought, and now there was real panic in her mind. He couldn't be normal to give that fierce grin and that fierce laugh.

'Tell you what,' he said, 'we'll find some shade to park in, and then we'll go off the road and have a little cuddle! How does that sound? We haven't been together for two whole nights!'

She felt as if she couldn't breathe properly.

'Good idea?' he asked, and turned a corner. To her dismay she saw that there was a wide stretch where cars could park, on the cliff-side of the road. No cars were parked there now. Narrow paths led off from the parking place towards the higher hills; it was obviously a well-used sightseeing spot.

Clive pulled in, and then drove to a little defile between some trees where there was a little shade.

'Plenty more shade up top,' he said, and grinned again. 'I promise you it's one of the loveliest sights in this part of the Alps. Nothing to compare with the Swiss Alps or even the French nearer the Swiss border, but around here they're really something.' He seemed to speak with less precision than before, rather as if a veneer of culture was wearing off. 'Don't look so shocked, sweetie—we *are* man and wife.'

A question came to the tip of her tongue, and she could not keep it back.

'Are we?'

'What the hell do you mean?' he snapped.

'I just wanted to be sure, Clive,' Gillian said quietly. 'You haven't let me see my passport once since we landed.'

'That's a man's job,' he said abruptly. 'You take the biscuit, you really do. Yesterday you thought I was running away from something, and today you suggest that I've fooled you. Well, you're wrong. We are legally man and wife according to French law, and that's good enough for other countries. It's certainly good enough for you. Haven't you seen the certificate?'

'Clive,' Gillian said, 'I would like to see my passport, please.'

'Fat lot of use that would be. Your passport isn't altered yet—you'll have to apply for a change of name, and it isn't necessary just yet. There's no law against being married out of England.'

'I'd like to see it, Clive.'

'So you would,' he said, and actually sneered. 'All right, so you shall.' He stretched out behind him, picked up his briefcase and tucked it under his arm; then he climbed out of the car. 'Let's go up into the woods for some shade, and I'll show it to you there.'

'Don't be silly, Clive.'

'I'm not silly,' he said. 'I'm just tired of the heat. I thought you were a few minutes ago. I'm damned if I know what to make of you. First you're hot, then you want to sit in a stewing car and look at passports. First you like the idea of shade, and then you won't walk for two minutes to get some. What's the matter with you?'

Gillian didn't answer.

'Oh, all right,' Macklin said. 'If the only thing that will satisfy you is your passport, you can see it.' He took out his keys, several of them in a small leather case, unlocked the briefcase, and delved inside. She watched tensely, and hotter than she could ever remember being. The shade of the trees just off the road seemed to beckon her, but her heart was beating very fast and at moments she felt as if it would choke her.

He handed her her passport. She turned over the pages. There was a note pinned to it, giving details of the marriage ceremony at Auxerre. It had a rubber stamp impression, showing the date, and naming the town of Auxerre. Everything seemed in order, and it could not have been more lucid—although the certificate itself wasn't there. She wondered whether she ought to ask to see it, or whether that would be going too far. The truth was that she had doubts of him, grave doubts which gave her a sick feeling whenever she thought of what she had done. But if he *had* married her, then what could be wrong? If everything was above-board. . . .

His eyes were very narrow as he looked at her and asked:

'Satisfied?'

'Yes, I suppose so,' she said.

'You suppose so! I tell you, you really take the biscuit. Gillian, what is all this about? Perhaps you doubt if *my* passport is in order.' He delved into the briefcase for what seemed a long time, apparently drawing things out, letting them go again, and trying something else. At last he snatched out a passport, exactly like hers to look at, and he thrust it towards her.

She immediately saw that it was not the one which he used at hotels.

This was new; that one was quite old.

She opened this new one, slowly, and looked at the details inside. The sight of his photograph made her draw in her breath; in it, he looked more like the man in England than like this brusque, aggressive person of the moment. Perhaps she was simply finding out how different a man was after marriage. Perhaps she was going to have to live with this kind of uncertainty all her life, never quite sure what mood he would be in. And—she had to admit that if everything was straightforward, then she must have been exasperating, to say the least.

But why had he given her this passport?

Should she ask to see the other?

That would bring about the biggest storm yet; she had no doubt about that. He seemed to be challenging her to question him further, and she could not make up her mind what to do.

'Satisfied?' he demanded curtly.

She would have to wait until she had an opportunity to see the other passport when he presented it at an hotel; there was nothing else to do. Out here in the scorching heat was no place for her to argue with him and try to force an issue.

'Yes, of course,' she made herself say, and closed her eyes. 'It must be the heat, Clive. I—I'm sorry.'

'Come and get some shade, and forget all about it,' he said with rough kindliness. 'I'll tell you what—get into those thicker sandals of yours, the paths are a bit rocky. It'll be more comfortable, and you'll give the others a chance to cool off. Right?'

'All—all right,' Gillian said.

He flung open the boot of the car, and pulled out the top case, which was hers, opened it, took out the sandals, and in a sudden excess of concern, made her sit on the edge of the boot while he took off her thin white shoes, and put on her sandals. He began to run his hands up and down the calves of her leg, and yesterday that would have seemed no more than a promise. Today, she did not like it. Today, she did not like him. That was the awful fact which she had to face: she did not like the man she had married.

He jumped up.

'Comfy?'

'Yes, thanks.'

'Come on then,' Clive cried. 'I'll carry you up the steep parts, and we'll soon be at the top. Hurry!'

His eyes were glittering and his voice was thick, as if he could not wait to get among the trees.

22

Heat

'I'VE never felt so hot,' Felicity said, and she looked as if that were true. Her face was red and her eyes were glassy. She sat back in her seat, staring out at the sun-drenched hills.

'Remember South Africa?'

'We're not in South Africa,' Felicity snapped. 'I almost wish we were.' Her voice was husky with anxiety. 'Pat, we're not going to find her.'

'It's too early to say that.'

'It's hopeless now. I can't help it, but I've just got to get out of this blazing sun and get cool.'

Dawlish said, 'Soon, Fel.'

'No, not soon. Now.'

'We can't,' Dawlish said simply. 'We haven't passed a parking place where there was any shade in the last hour.'

'I didn't realize that it got so hot up here.'

'You've never had a journey like this with two nights without real sleep,' Dawlish said quietly. 'I'm beginning to feel it, too.'

'You must be half dead.'

'I'll be all right. Fel——'

'Pat, I know what you feel, I know you're absolutely *driven* to try to find this Gillian, but it's no use fighting against human nature. We're absolutely exhausted. If we don't get some rest soon we'll both crack up, and that won't help anyone.'

Dawlish didn't speak.

It was two hours since they had pushed the car over the

cliff—two burning hours. The sun seemed pitiless. All the colour was bleached out of the trees, the leaves of which dropped listlessly. Now and again they saw the flat bed of a great river, almost dry except in the middle of the course; great rocks, boulders and trees lay on the river bed, where a torrent had dragged them and left them, and had died. It seemed as if nothing could live in this heat, and Felicity felt as if she were sitting in an oven with the gas being turned up all the time.

'Pat . . .'

'We'll have a breather soon, darling.'

'For heaven's sake be sensible! A breather's no use to us.'

'We can't stop here,' Dawlish said stubbornly.

Felicity didn't answer, just leaned back and tried to close her eyes, but they were prickly with the heat and even more uncomfortable closed than open. Every window was wide open, but the air which came in seemed to be hotter than the air already in the car. Now and again they passed another car, but there was nothing parked by the side of the road: everyone seemed to be driving fast to get out of the mountains and the aridness.

They turned a wide corner. Ahead the road seemed wider and there was a big area gouged out of the rock, with a fringe of trees around it; beneath the trees were black spots of shade.

'Pat, we can go there!'

'It's not shady enough,' Dawlish said. 'We wouldn't——'

'We could park the car and get out for an hour. Pat, I tell you I can't stand this heat any longer.'

Dawlish said quietly, 'I'm sorry, Fel, but you've got to. We can't give up now. We're less than twenty miles from Gap, and we'll be at Digne in less than an hour.'

'As soon as you get there you'll want to go on somewhere else.'

'I don't know where else to go.'

'Oh, you'll guess! Pat, I'm not fooling. I shall faint right out if we go on any longer. I must have a rest under some shade. I can't help it.'

'All right,' Dawlish said, and after a moment he went on, 'The next place we come to I'll drop you, and come back for you when I've got as far as Digne.'

'Don't be silly!'

'Fel, you aren't being exactly reasonable, are you?' Dawlish said, his voice tensing. 'I know it's hot. I also feel that girl may be somewhere between here and Digne, and that the only chance she's got is for us to try to find her.'

'You can't be sure we'll be able to help her!'

'We can be sure that no one else can.'

'The police——'

'If the police had found her we would have heard by now.'

'They ought to have done more.'

'Possibly,' Dawlish said. 'It would be a help if they knew what car they were looking for, and what name Macklin's travelling under. There hasn't been time.'

'It's always the same, it's never been any different since I've known you,' said Felicity shrilly. 'The only one who can do anything is the great Patrick Dawlish. The police are no use, Scotland Yard's no use, all France is no use—the only man with any sense and the only man who can do anything is Patrick Dawlish. But you're wrong, don't you understand? You're wrong. It's a waste of time—this is one occasion when you aren't any help to anyone.'

Dawlish said, 'All right, Fel.'

'And don't just sit there turning the other cheek!'

'Fel,' Dawlish said, his voice brittle, 'it hasn't been good for either of us. Just hold tight for half an hour or so longer, and you can stay at an hotel in Digne while I look around with the police. We know that Macklin was heading this way, we took the only reasonable road, and the chances are that he isn't far away from here.'

'You don't even know that he's heading for Digne; you only guessed it.'

Dawlish didn't speak.

They were driving fast along a straight stretch of road with the river on one side, the sun reflecting from it dazzlingly, and the cliff rising almost sheer on the other. A car came tearing towards them, a great cloud of dust hanging behind it. A long way ahead they saw a patch of trees on the river side. Felicity sat up, staring towards it. Dawlish began to slow down. The trees were large and the shade they cast spread halfway across the road; there was plenty of room for the car to stand in the shade, and on the instant it seemed cooler.

'Take the water bottle and one of the folding chairs,' Dawlish said, 'and I'll be back as soon as I can.'

'Don't be absurd. You've got to rest, too.'

'Fel, I can't,' Dawlish said very quietly. 'I don't want to live with the thought that I might have stopped that girl from being killed in the way that boy at Fontainebleau was killed. It's no use arguing, and there isn't time to waste.' He leaned across and opened her door.

Felicity leaned back and closed her eyes, very close to tears.

'I can't stay here alone,' she said hopelessly. 'You'd better go on.'

. . . . .

'Well,' Macklin said, 'what do you think of the view from here?'

'It's wonderful,' Gillian agreed.

They stood hundreds of feet above the road, looking over the mountains, seeing the bed of the river a long way below, the stones bleached nearly white, and the narrow stream in the middle glittering like silver touched with gold. They could see the road, too, but it was almost vertically beneath them. There was the shade of small trees here, and there were stones which could be used as seats. Odds and ends of paper and cartons were strewn about as this was a well-used picnic spot.

'There's just one more place,' Macklin said.

'Clive, I think I'd like to go back to the car now.'

'We can walk round this way and get back to it,' he promised her. 'It won't be long.'

'All right,' Gillian conceded.

His arm was round her, and she wished that it was not. For one thing, his arm and his body were very warm, and it was much too hot. For another, he kept shivering; he had little spasms of absolutely uncontrollable shivers, and although neither of them spoke of that, it puzzled her. Obviously Clive could not be unaware of them. As they turned away from this spot he had one.

'It's so hot,' Gillian said.

'Don't you want my arm round you, eh, lover?'

'It's only because it's so hot, Clive.'

'I wonder,' said Clive. He gave a little high-pitched laugh. 'Never mind. That way.' He pointed towards a narrow path which led steeply up a hill, with trees on either side. Obviously he knew the place quite well. She did not want to climb any higher because she was tired and too hot, and because she was frightened. She could not understand him at all. Now and again he fell against her, stumbling, and apologized. Now and again she caught him looking at her oddly. She had never felt so much on edge, and she began to long to get back to the car and to the road where there would be other people.

She reached the crest of the hill.

It was superbly beautiful, for the tops of mountains stretched out almost as far as she could see in each direction. And a long way down there was the ribbon of road; it turned a hairpin bend almost immediately beneath them and disappeared from view. But the most astonishing thing was the cliff edge straight in front of her. It looked as if it had been sliced off with a knife. The drop was sheer for several hundred feet, and beneath it was a kind of fissure, as if the axe had finished down there, cleaving the earth in two. It was at once exciting and frightening; if anyone should fall down there they would be lost for weeks, perhaps for ever. Once down in that fissure there would be no getting out.

'Do I know my France?' asked Clive in a choky voice.

'Yes, it's wonderful,' Gillian said. 'If only it weren't so hot I'd love it.'

'Don't turn away,' Clive said. 'Just look at the view.'

'Clive, I've seen it. I'd like——'

'*Look over there!*' he exclaimed in a high-pitched voice, and pointed towards the river. She was so startled that she did what he said, and looked at the river, the white rocks, the dark greenery and the empty sky. 'What——' she began, and then she felt him push her.

In that moment she knew the truth.

She was right on the edge of that sheer cliff, and his hands were between her shoulders, pushing hard. Terror flared up in her. She felt herself tottering forward. She screamed and the sound seemed lost. She tried to move to one side, but he stopped her with a rough grab at her arm.

'Clive, what are you doing?' she cried. 'Clive!' She turned her head and saw the glitter in his eyes and knew exactly what to expect: no mercy at all. 'Don't, don't push me over!' she screamed. 'Clive!' Yet he was pushing her roughly, and although she leaned all her weight against his hands she couldn't stop herself from staggering forward; she hadn't any chance at all. 'Help!' she screamed to the empty sky. '*Help, help, help!*' She tottered forward again, and now seemed to be leaning over the side of the cliff and staring down into the valley where a body might lie for ever. 'Clive, don't,' she sobbed. 'Don't kill me, don't kill me!' But he was going to kill her, and she could not kick backwards at him because if she were on one foot only for a moment she would fall over. 'Please let me go,' she pleaded, 'Clive!'

It was useless.

But just below, and a little to the right, there was a ledge. And if she could get on that ledge and be free from him she might be able to run and lose herself in the trees. Oh, God, help her. That pressure against her shoulders was more remorseless than ever, and she could hear Clive gasping for breath.

Then she darted forward and pushed him. He slipped and staggered, and she stumbled on. If she slipped in turn, she would fall and die; but if she could reach that ledge there was hope.

23

Over

GILLIAN felt herself toppling forward as she ran, and for awful seconds was afraid she would not be able to save herself. She tried to veer to the right, but the slope was steeper than she had expected. She was sobbing for breath and the terror was white hot in her.

She flung herself towards the ledge.

In the middle of it was a small bush which had seemed tiny from some distance off, but now seemed larger. She thrust her whole weight towards it and grabbed. Thorns tore into her fingers, but she held on. It checked her fall, and for a moment she was standing still and upright—safe. The steep drop lay behind her, but for a moment she was out of Clive's reach.

She took a step sideways and let go of the bush; her fingers were bleeding badly from the scratches. She glanced round and saw Clive some distance away; she could dodge to either side if he came on, and he would be in risk of falling if he lunged at her. It was only a temporary haven, but there was just a chance that she could get among the trees and lose Clive. Oh, dear God, why was he doing this to her?

She turned again, and felt a sharp thud at her waist, and it jolted her forward. A big stone dropped on to the ledge and bounced over. Another hurtled past her head.

'Stop it!' she screamed.

She began to run along the ledge towards the trees. It was steeper even than she had realized, and she kept stumbling. She did not know whether Clive was throwing more stones or not; he was still behind her, and she dared only look ahead. The trees seemed a long way off and there were great gaps between them; she couldn't hide, but she might be able to run far enough to dodge him, might be able to get down to the road. Any path would take her.

She reached the first of the trees, with the steep hillside on her right, the sheer drop on her left.

A stone struck the trunk, rebounded, and dropped on her foot. She gasped with pain and had to stop. She put one hand against the tree, and lifted her right foot and clutched it. She twisted round so that she could see Clive, and he was following her some distance up the hillside, obviously intent on cutting her off. There was no doubt that he would kill her if once he got his hands on her again, and he was moving much faster than she could. In a few moments he would be on the ledge in front of her, and she wouldn't be able to get past. She tried to walk. Her ankle almost gave way, and she knew that it had been badly bruised. She clenched her teeth and tried again, and nearly fell. So she couldn't get away from him.

But she must try to fight.

Obviously he realized that she could not get away. So he was slowing down. He was looking at her all the time, and his lips were bared in the strange way she had noticed several times in the car. She saw the glitter in his eyes. She wondered how she could ever have fallen in love with this man, and wondered what awful thing had turned him into a murderer, whether he had planned her murder from the time they had set out from London.

Could that be true?

If it was, then *why?*

He was saying something; he was calling out to her. He was still fifty yards away, but no matter whether she went right or left he could cut her off, and if she went back it would be to the yawning cliff.

'*Gillian!*'

She didn't answer. She wanted a weapon of some kind,

but could see nothing. Stones and rocks were useless to her, she simply couldn't throw; and her ankle seemed as if it were on fire every time she touched the ground with her right foot. She was gasping for breath, and yet she did not feel the panic that she had a few minutes before; there was the chance to fight.

'Gillian!'

There was nothing at hand except stones. She stood there, resting against a tree, and then bent down and picked up two heavy stones, and knew that she would not be able to throw them more than a few yards.

'Gillian! It's all right, I won't hurt you! Don't run away from me any more.'

Did he think she was mad?

'I don't know what came over me,' he called. His forehead and his face were streaming with sweat, and he kept moistening his lips. 'You needn't worry, I won't hurt you.'

He would kill her.

'Don't come any nearer,' she cried, but she doubted whether her voice was loud enough to reach him. 'Stay away!' she went on desperately, and her voice broke; but he heard her that time.

'Gillian, you needn't worry. It—it must have been a stroke or something. I'll help you to get down, I'll do anything I can for you. Don't keep running away.'

'*Don't come any nearer!*'

But he was nearer, and his glittering eyes told the truth: that he would kill her the moment he reached her, and that there were only minutes between life and death, for no matter how she fought, she could not overpower him.

He drew nearer.

'It's all right,' he called. 'I swear it.'

She could not dart through right or left; she could not put her weight on that ankle. She could hobble backwards, that was all: towards the edge of the cliff.

And then, from a long way below, there came the blare of a car horn.

. . . . .

Dawlish and Felicity had not exchanged a word from the moment Dawlish had driven on from the shadow by the river. He knew that when she had rested she would wish she had not behaved like this, but he could not blame her; his own nerves were at breaking point, and it was worse because there was no certainty that they could find the girl, no certainty even that she was near here. It was stubbornness more than hope that made him go on.

They turned a corner at a great sweep in the nearly dried-up river. On the side of the road beneath the cliffs was a wide clearing, with ample room to park, and a number of paths led up to the top of the cliffs. A bright blue car stood out of the glare of the sun, some distance off, in a narrow opening where there was some shade. A little way up the hillside there were trees and precious shade. Dawlish pulled off the road and drew up near the other car, a Simca, the boot lid of which was open an inch or two.

'What good will this do?' Felicity made herself ask.

'Sooner or later we'll catch up with them,' Dawlish said. 'Fel, don't——'

'All right,' she said more easily. 'I'm sorry, Pat. I know you're right, but don't expect any sense from me.'

He gave her a quick bright smile and got out. The sun seemed to strike savagely at him; it was a much fiercer heat than inside the car. He eased his collar as he went to the back of the Simca. He did not really expect to find what he was looking for; it was more a forlorn hope than a serious attempt. He pushed the boot lid up further, saw three cases jammed in it, a pair of white shoes on one side, a few travelling oddments pushed between the cases. He looked at the label, and read: *Miss G. Kelvedon.* For a moment he stared at it stupidly, as he did at the letters *G. K.* on the side of another case.

G. K.

'*Fel!*' he bellowed. 'We've found them!'

She was staring at him out of the window, astounded as he. He snatched off the label and strode to her, his eyes blazing, fatigue completely forgotten.

'It's hers!' he shouted. 'Fel, they're somewhere nearby. We've found——'

'*Quiet!*' Felicity cried.

He stopped.

There was only the stillness of the afternoon and the fierceness of the heat and the humming of insects—until all that was broken by a high-pitched cry, words which were indistinguishable but which carried an unmistakable shrill note of alarm.

'What is that?' Felicity asked in a hushed voice.

Dawlish was staring upwards towards the trees, knowing that whoever was up there might be to the left or right, might be a hundred or a thousand yards away, sounds travelled so clearly in this clear air.

Two words came faintly: 'Stop it!'

Then there was silence.

'I'm going up,' Dawlish said tensely. 'Stay here, and if any more cars come by stop them and send the men up after me.' He was already moving. 'Give me about three minutes, and then keep blowing the horn. If Macklin thinks there's someone about he won't be so likely to take risks.'

Felicity was scrambling out of the car.

'All right, but hurry!'

Dawlish ran across the clearing towards one of the paths, and she had never seen him move faster. He leapt up the path, grabbing at trees to keep his balance. He disappeared. She heard the sound of his progress, thought she heard the scream again, but it was fainter and she could not be sure. She was hardly aware now of the sun, only of the possibility that they might be too late even now.

There were no sounds now; no cars came; only the sun shone on the parched land and the withered trees and the distant river bed.

She leaned inside the Lagonda, pressed the horn, and kept on pressing.

. . . . .

Dawlish heard the sound clearly, before he had seen either the man or the girl. In his mind there was the dread in case he had arranged for that alarm too soon. He could hear nothing else, and it was going on and on. He wanted the girl or man to shout again, but neither of them had, and he had waited until now in the hope of getting near enough to take the man by surprise, but he began to fear that he had left it too long.

The girl might be dead.

The silence might mean that Macklin had killed her.

The screech of the horn faded.

'Gillian!' bellowed Dawlish. 'Shout as loud as you can.'

He heard nothing.

'Shout as loud as you can!' he cried.

Then he heard a sound, the beginning of a cry; but immediately it was broken off, and there was a different noise, as of scuffling.

'I'm coming!' Dawlish roared, and raced through the trees in the direction of the sound; the sound itself was the one thing which guided him. Then the horn below blared out again, and he could not hear anything up here. 'Fel, stop it!' he said aloud in desperation. 'Oh, God, stop it!' The horn stopped. The scuffling was still going on nearby, and then he heard a woman cry!

'*This way!*'

He swung towards his left. There was a narrow path leading upwards sharply, and he jumped to the top, and stopped for a second, not really seeing the beautiful panorama stretching out in front of him, but seeing the cliffside which looked as if an axe had been wielded by a giant to carve it in two. He saw the man and the girl some distance to the right, struggling.

They were very near the edge of the cliff, not far along. He could not hope to reach them in time to drag the man away from the girl. She was clinging desperately to the trunk of a tree, and if the man once prised her loose she would almost certainly fall.

Dawlish shouted, 'All right! I'm coming!' and began to run. First he had to get to a ledge, and he knew that if he slipped or if the earth gave way under his weight he would not have a chance, but nor would the girl, without him. He reached the ledge. He saw the man look round. He recognized madness there, if only the madness of fear. He saw the man draw back from the girl, who was half-crouching by the tree and still clinging to it. The man stood without moving for what seemed a long time.

'Stay just where you are,' Dawlish called. He was gulping for breath, but knew that he had saved the girl; Macklin would not harm her. He took his automatic from his pocket, showed it, and kept Macklin covered. 'Don't move,' he called again, and then said to Gillian, 'You're quite safe; you've nothing to worry about.'

Then Macklin moved.

He did not try to touch the girl and he did not attempt to run past, for he must know that he would be shot down. He ran towards the edge of the cliff. The girl saw him and her mouth dropped open. Dawlish saw the desperation on Macklin's face, and knew that the man had come to his final decision.

He leapt over the side, and as he disappeared from sight he did not even scream.

When Dawlish reached Gillian she was sobbing helplessly.

Down below the car horn was screeching, but it did not matter. Dawlish held the girl closely as he carried her down, and neither of them tried to speak. He reached one of the main paths, and two men came into sight, youngsters in open-necked shirts, who stopped at sight of him until Dawlish said:

'Carry her between you, will you?' They came eagerly, two English youths on holiday, and Dawlish swayed a little when Gillian's weight was gone, and then followed as the others carried her in a chair made by their arms, towards the clearing, the cars and Felicity.

. . . . .

Seven hours later Macklin's body was brought up. By that time Mrs. Kelvedon was flying from London, Felicity and Gillian were sleeping in a cool hotel room at Digne, and Dawlish was talking to the local police after a long telephone talk with Corot. The main burden of that talk was simply that the police now knew what Macklin had been doing and had found many if not most of his contacts, but they still did not know why he had set out to kill the girl.

24

Hidden Factor

'I'M not very good at using words,' Mrs. Kelvedon said, 'but I shall never be able to thank you, Mr. Dawlish. To the end of my days I shall be grateful.' She spoke very quietly, her voice a little husky as she sat in a boudoir next to the room where Felicity and Gillian lay sleeping.

Dawlish, who had snatched his sleep, both looked and felt much better. He did not smile at Mrs. Kelvedon as she spoke, and appeared to be watching her intently, as if there were something heavily on his mind.

'I hope you'll believe that,' Mrs. Kelvedon went on. 'It may sound old-fashioned, but for the rest of your life you will have this mother's blessing.'

'Yes,' Dawlish said. 'I'm sure.'

'And Gillian will feel the same, too.'

'Ah,' said Dawlish. 'Gillian. She has a lot to worry about, hasn't she?'

'Not really,' Gillian's mother answered. 'Not now, Mr. Dawlish. She's very young, and the young soon forget even the most unpleasant experiences.'

'I wonder.'

'You should know they do.'

'It depends how unpleasant and whom it involves,' said Dawlish. 'If someone of whom one is tremendously fond conspires to kill——'

'But she'll forget him,' Mrs. Kelvedon interrupted quickly. She was leaning forward in her chair overlooking the sweeping lawns of the hotel and the rose garden near the window. The room was beautifully appointed, with the kind of furniture which Macklin had bought and sold. 'I'm sure she will, Mr. Dawlish—after all, she is only twenty-three.

Many a girl has practically forgotten her first husband. I don't want to turn this into too great a tragedy.'

'I can believe it,' Dawlish said.

Gillian's mother was strikingly handsome, and he was reminding himself of that as he studied her. There was something of Gillian about her eyes and her forehead, but otherwise they were not really alike. She wore a dark blue silk suit, her greying hair was beautifully groomed, and the fear had gone out of her eyes; but Dawlish remembered when he had first met her, and could remember the fear she had shown then.

'I don't quite understand you,' she said.

'I don't suppose you do,' Dawlish replied, and for the first time he smiled. 'I believe that Gillian will forget Macklin, although it might take longer than you think. There will always be the deep scar of memory of a man she thought she loved, and who tried to kill her. But there's a worse one in store for her, isn't there?'

'I repeat, I just don't understand you,' Mrs. Kelvedon said, but now there was a wary look in her eyes. 'Is there something you haven't told me about? Something even worse than I know?'

'You know,' declared Dawlish.

'Mr. Dawlish, I wish you wouldn't speak in riddles,' Mrs. Kelvedon protested. She stood up from her chair and went to the window, staring out on to the lawn as if she no longer wanted to face him. 'Will you please tell me exactly what you mean?'

'Yes,' said Dawlish. He stood up and joined her. The fear was back in her eyes, and there was tension in her body. 'Macklin was one of many agents, of course. He called regularly on certain antique and second-hand shops, there is no doubt that he handled drugs as well as stolen valuables, and there's little doubt that he knew only some of the shops and some of the people involved. How many more do you know, Mrs. Kelvedon?'

'Are you serious?' The fear flared up in her eyes.

'Very,' said Dawlish quietly. 'No, don't turn away; try

looking at me. Because I've an unpleasant decision to make,' Dawlish went on. 'I'd like to be sure that it's the right one. You knew that Gillian had been sent out of the country, and you knew the truth about Macklin, didn't you?'

Mrs. Kelvedon didn't answer, but all the colour had drained from her face.

'You knew that she was in grave danger, and you dared not tell the police why,' Dawlish went on stonily. 'You hoped that by getting me to go after Gillian I might save her, and so might save your face. Because if the police had probed too deeply they would have discovered that you were also one of the agents, and that you would be liable to a very long term of imprisonment if you were found out. And your employer or a colleague sent Gillian away—your employer, presumably, since you couldn't prevent him. You were afraid that Gillian might be killed, and so you came to me. You believed that if I were trying to help her there would be less danger of her being killed, didn't you? You didn't know your employer well enough.'

Only the woman's eyes had any colour now.

'Tell me,' asked Dawlish quietly, 'did you know that Ivy Marshall had gone the same way?'

Mrs. Kelvedon cried, in awful desperation, 'Oh, God, I didn't dream you would find this out, but you're right. I found out about Ivy, that's why I had to do something. I——' She broke off, her face working, but Dawlish did not speak, and she went on in a trembling voice:

'I—I knew that Gillian was being drawn into a criminal organization; I tried to prevent it, but the—the man in charge of it sent her away. He said that Macklin was in love with her, promised she would be all right, but——'

She broke off again.

'Who promised you that?' asked Dawlish. 'How much do you know, Kay? I've an ugly feeling that you weighed your own safety against the life of your daughter, and you put yourself way out in front. You sent me after her as a kind of salve to your conscience, precious little more. And the decision I have to make is whether to tell Gillian or not.'

Mrs. Kelvedon drew in a sharp breath which seemed to hurt her.

'You can't,' she said hoarsely. 'You couldn't be so cruel.'

'You should have heard her screaming, and you should have seen her clinging to the trunk of a tree in a desperate effort to save her life.'

'*Don't!*'

'Don't you like looking at yourself?' asked Dawlish icily.

'I didn't know! I was promised she would be all right; it wasn't until after she had gone that I realized that I had to find someone to save her. I tell you I had absolute confidence in you.'

Dawlish said, 'I can tell Gillian all this when she comes round, or I can tell the police. They'll find out the whole truth sooner or later anyhow. If you refuse to tell me I shall tell them everything I can—everything I've guessed from the time you were so insistent that I should keep away from the police. I couldn't understand why, at the time, and that really pointed the way to the truth. Who is it?'

'I can't tell you,' she said. 'It's no use. He would kill——'

'He can't, now.'

'You don't know him!'

Dawlish said, 'If you name him, I'll name him to the police. No one will know that the information came from you. He'll be under arrest within a few hours. I can say that Macklin named him—no one need ever know differently. Once he's under arrest he will never be free to do you any harm. Who is he, Kay?'

'Oh, God!' she gasped, 'I can't tell you!'

'Then I shall tell Gillian that you know a great deal.'

'You can't!'

'There isn't a hope for you unless you name the man,' Dawlish said, 'and whether there's any hope for you if you do so is out of my hands. I won't name you, once you've named him. If he doesn't name you, you'll be all right. Do you think he'll give you away, simply out of spite?'

She didn't answer, and there were tears in her eyes; it was strange and almost repugnant to see a woman of her age and her striking attractiveness sobbing.

'Kay,' Dawlish said, 'you've been a widow for many years. You might reasonably expect a lonely life. You know that Gillian won't share your life with you much longer. But you aren't old. You're in the early forties and an extremely attractive woman as well as one of great vitality. I can't see you living a spinster's life—I don't think you have, for a long time. Is it the man you hope to marry? Is that what's holding you back now, and is that what made you ready to sacrifice Gillian?'

She drew a sharp breath, as if the suggestion hurt her.

'Would you like time to think about it?' Dawlish asked quietly. 'You can have a little while. The one thing you can't have is an opportunity to warn the man and give him a chance to get away.'

'How long can I have?' asked Gillian's mother.

'How long would you like?'

She hesitated and turned to look at the roses again. Dawlish saw the tears glistening in her eyes, and could not fail to notice the natural pride with which she held her fine body.

Without looking at him she said, 'It won't make any difference now, I suppose. You mean what you say.' Dawlish murmured 'Yes,' and after a moment's hesitation the woman went on: 'His name is Sharp—Andrew Sharp, the antique dealer in London. I've worked with him for many years, and have been his mistress for nearly a year. I believed that one day we would get married. I had no idea he was a criminal until after he had been using my shop for a long time—and even when I found out, I was too fond of him to think seriously of going to the police at first. But I began to worry about Ivy Marshall's murder, for she had worked at one of Sharp's shops, from which I knew he sold stolen goods.' As she said this, Gillian's mother turned to look at Dawlish, and her voice hardened. 'Something Sharp said about making sure Ivy wasn't a danger—he'd had too much to drink one evening—made me wonder what had really happened.

'I taxed Sharp with knowing about the murder and he denied it convincingly,' Kay Kelvedon went on. 'I'd already arranged to go away for a holiday because I was nervy and tired, and went to Penzance. It didn't occur to me that I'd seriously worried Sharp, or that he would kidnap Gillian until I came back and found her gone. But then I had a terrible moment when I remembered that before I knew about the crimes, Gillian had found a kind of hiding place in an old Regency chair, and I'd told Sharp about it. I was terrified, and I accused Sharp wildly of being behind Gillian's disappearance. He admitted that he was. I know you'll think I should have gone to the police right away, Pat, but he told me he would make sure she never came back alive if I went to them. And I'd no proof, no proof at all.'

Kay Kelvedon paused as if overcome by the recollection, and it was a long time before she went on:

'He frightened me; that's the simple truth. There was a very big deal in stolen miniatures and antique jewellery coming off three weeks after Gillian disappeared, and he needed my help. I had to sell most of the goods through my shop. Sharp said that when it was done Gillian would come back—said that he *had* to make me compliant for at least three weeks and had sent Gillian out of the country so as to make sure of me. I was absolutely desperate by then.' Kay's voice began to break as she went on. 'You can imagine how dreadful I felt when Sharp told me that Gillian had gone with Macklin—the man who had taken Ivy Marshall out of England. Pat, you must believe me when I say that I was positive that Gillian would be murdered if I went to the police. I even thought he would only keep her alive as long as he needed me. He'd never intended marriage, of course, only wanted me as a cover to his activities. I thought both Gillian and I were in danger, I dared not go to the police—so, you were my one hope.'

Gillian's mother stopped and waited for Dawlish's reaction, as if she feared the worst.

'All right,' he said quietly. 'I shall tell the police that before Macklin killed himself I heard him shout Sharp's name. I won't tell Gillian any of this. Whether you'll be able to live with her without her knowing . . .' he left the sentence in mid-air. 'I'll leave you to work that out. Do you think Sharp will name you?'

'If he thinks it will help him, he certainly will,' Mrs. Kelvedon answered bitterly. 'I've learned what a cold-blooded devil he is, and I've also learned to hate him. But Pat, when you came into this room I told you that I should never be able to thank you. That is more true now than ever.' She raised her hands in front of her breast almost pleadingly. 'Please believe that. And believe that if I'd realized earlier that Gillian would be in any real danger I would have gone to the police. By the time I knew, her danger was too great.'

'I've seldom wanted to believe anything as much as I want to believe that,' Dawlish told her.

25

Future . . .

'DARLING!' Felicity called.

'Hallo, sweet, what is it?'

'Can you come?'

'Give me two minutes,' said Dawlish.

He was pulling a roller across the lawn of his house in Surrey, after a morning of rain which made the turf exactly right for rolling. It was a late afternoon in September, the sun was shining brightly, although much of its warmth had gone. The pseudo-Tudor house looked picturesque enough to be genuine, the trees and bushes round it were well fed with rain, and it seemed a world away from the Alpes Maritimes—as it was. He finished rolling, tugged the roller back to a shed near the house, and then strolled in the back way, wiping his feet on the thick mat at the back door. He heard Felicity hurrying. She looked excited, and she looked lovely, and she looked very well.

'What's it all about?' Dawlish asked.

'We're going to have two extras for dinner—Tim and Joan are coming.'

Dawlish's face lit up. 'What time will they be here?'

'About half-past six,' Felicity said, and her eyes were glowing as she looked at Dawlish's massive figure. He knew there was much more on her mind than she had yet said. 'Pat——'

'You have the look of a guilty secret,' Dawlish said with mock severity.

'I have,' confessed Felicity. 'Guilt, if not a secret. I never think of Gillian Kelvedon without thinking that if you'd listened to me we would have been too late.'

'Forget it, darling.'

'I doubt if I ever shall,' declared Felicity. 'Ted told me that she's got a job in the United States, and her mother's encouraged her to go.'

'Well, well,' said Dawlish. 'That's exactly right for her.'

'I always had a feeling that there was something about that case that you kept to yourself,' Felicity said. 'Was there?'

'What a shocking thought.'

'So there was,' said Felicity musingly. 'I suppose you'll tell me what it was when it suits you. The queer thing about the whole affair was that it started so simply—I wouldn't have said a word to encourage you to go if I'd known that it was going to be a really big investigation. How many people worked for that man Sharp?'

'The last police list of agents was a hundred and seventeen,' Dawlish told her.

'And he shipped the drugs and everything else he dealt in, in the furniture with hollow legs and hollow seats and tops, and in picture frames and *objets d'art*?'

'The lot,' Dawlish agreed.

'It was a pity he couldn't be hanged for the murder of Ivy Marshall,' Felicity said, 'but at least he got fifteen years in prison. Pat . . .'

'Hm?'

'I don't think I'll ever forget shouting at you in the car that afternoon. I suppose my nerves had gone all to pieces after the fright on the mountain road, and what with the heat and everything——No, don't stop me!' She fended him off. 'I've always wanted to say that I hate myself for what I said to you. *Don't*. I don't believe that anyone else could have saved Gillian. I don't think there's another man who——'

She had to stop because he was holding her so tightly.

'It's going to be tough on Kay Kelvedon when Gillian goes,' Joan Beresford said at dinner that night. 'But Gillian tells me that if it hadn't been for her mother, she wouldn't have had the offer of the job. She'll have to be over there for three years, so she'll probably marry an American—it's hard to believe she actually *was* married, isn't it?'

Felicity agreed that it was.

Tim Beresford said, in his deep voice, that not many girls were so fortunate in their mothers as Gillian Kelvedon. Felicity was looking rather speculatively at Dawlish, who winked, helped himself to more cream for a raspberry mousse, and gave a loud, 'Hear, hear!'